Advance Praise for *Stories of Gabriel*

"In *Stories of Gabriel*, Esther Alix's debut fiction, a stillborn child unravels the many hidden, layered truths that are tightly woven into one Bronx community. Alix is a master storyteller, who in six interwoven stories pulls those who choose to follow down the hallways, and into the kitchens, and up onto the terraces of a Bronx block where news travels fast and secrets die hard. In *Gabriel* we see how a sudden trauma in one family can unwrap the collective pain, and grief, and heartbreak—as well as the resilience, and love, and longing—we all carry as individuals, and as families, and as communities. Alix has painted a remarkable and moving portrait of an endangered American institution—a real neighborhood, with very real people, forced to face the truth about each other and themselves."
—Frank Haberle, author of *Shufflers*

"Hauntingly beautiful snapshots of life that remain with you, long after the final page."
—Christopher Murphy, author of *The Other Side of the Mirror*

"*Stories of Gabriel* by Esther Alix is a sensory experience, inviting the reader into a vibrant world sitting at the intersection of New York City and Santo Domingo, populated by characters who are real, yet larger than life. I found myself wanting to be their friend. I want us to drink coffee and smoke cigarettes at my kitchen table. I want to cry and laugh with them in this marvelous debut that will leave you wanting more."
—Lana Garland, producer, *The Passing On*

Stories
of
Gabriel

Stories

of

Gabriel

Esther Alix

 Heliotrope Books

New York

Heliotrope Books LLC
heliotropebooks@gmail.com

ISBN: 978-1-942762-56-0
ISBN: 978-1-942762-55-3 eBook

Cover Art by Llanor Alleyne

Designed and typeset by Malcolm Fisher and Jonny Warschauer

For Mami

CONTENTS

Cafecito

Domingo stepped out onto his terrace into the warm spring air. He stared into the distance at the four squat, orange brick buildings in their horseshoe-shaped plaza. His building faced its twin, and each apartment in the complex had a terrace. He and his wife, Elli, lived on the third floor, and if the terrace doors were open and the lights were on, he could see directly into his neighbor's apartments. Matilda, the young woman across the way, was on the terrace combing her very long hair as she did most warm mornings. Her husband, Jorge, came up behind her and handed her a glass of water. Jorge kissed her gently on her forehead. Jorge spotted Domingo and waved before he stepped back inside his apartment. Matilda smiled, and Domingo waved and smiled back. This, he realized, had become part of his morning ritual since his retirement a few years ago. He glanced at the terrace adjacent to Jorge and Matilda's, but the door was closed, and the curtains pulled shut.

Petra, the old lady who lived on the second floor, under Matilda and Jorge, had been up all night, watching for her son. She stopped her vigil when she saw him walking up the block. She stepped into the apartment and closed the terrace door behind her. The son, rarely seen, worked nights, and his mother kept the same schedule as he did. Sometimes, if Domingo woke up early on a Saturday or

Sunday around three or four and glanced out the window, they'd be out there—mother and son playing cards,
drinking Miller Lite, and talking in whispers. Domingo
never learned the son's name. When the old lady sat out
there alone in the spring and summer nights waiting for
him, she would read romance novels with her back to the
window, where a bright light shined onto the terrace and
the book. She never acknowledged Domingo in any way.

The middle-aged couple that lived above Matilda and
Jorge were his favorite neighbors. Darren and his wife
ate dinner out on the terrace every night they could. From
what Domingo could see, Darren did all the cooking while
his wife, Frannie, sat reading magazines. They rarely came
out in the mornings, but once they got home from work,
the terrace door would open and stay open until they headed into the bedroom. After dinner, Darren would set up
the TV outside, and often, he and Domingo, both Yankees
fans, would yell out about the same play. Domingo would
be listening on the radio. They would look out at each other, wave, and laugh. If the Yankees weren't playing, they
would follow the Mets game.

Then Domingo turned to look toward 163rd Street,
near the empty lot where the Mexicans held the Virgin de
Guadalupe Feast Day celebration, and thought he saw *her*.
The sway of the floral skirt, the wrist full of bangles, and
the large purse she held, not on her shoulder, but in her
hand, as though it were a shopping bag. His breath caught
and his heart beat fast as he gripped the terrace railing.
It had been years since he had seen *her*. He straightened
his shoulders and braced himself for the liquid green of
her eyes.

The closer she came, the harder his old eyes focused.
There was something different about her. The swing of her
hips seemed less violent, the lips were full and red, and the
hair looked tamed. He reached for his glasses that were
perched on his head and put them on. The woman's face
was nice, wide, pretty; the lips sensuous; the hair long,
black, and full of waves. It wasn't *her*. He was both relieved

and disappointed. He felt like a fool, but still, he whispered her name. *Caro*lina. Caro*lina*. CAROLINA.

He was startled to see Elli walk onto the terrace, the smell of coffee wafting around her. She placed two chipped coffee cups on the small table between them. He sat, quickly embarrassed that he could get worked up with the thought of Carolina. He looked at his wife of almost forty-five years as she settled in the rocking chair across from him to read the *Daily Word* and felt weak and small.

Elli put down her prayer book, took a sip of coffee, and watched the early morning workers in the plaza. As she placed her cup down on the table between them, Domingo picked up his, and their hands brushed against each other. She looked up, half-smiled at him, put down her cup, and went back to reading. He watched her for a moment. Her hair was thinner; its deep brown color had faded to a light brown; wrinkles had gathered around her eyes and mouth, but her cheeks looked smooth, and her lips still had a bright, pink luster to them. Her fair skin was full of freckles; he particularly liked the ones on the bridge of her pudgy nose.

"Qué?" she said when she realized he was staring at her.

"Nada, nada," he said. It had been a long time, but he wondered if he had made it up to her, if she had truly forgiven him. He had not forgiven himself.

"Who did they take yesterday?" Elli asked as she stood, placing the small prayer book into her housecoat pocket and dangling her glasses between her thumb and forefinger. She leaned against the railing and looked toward the closed terrace door on the third floor.

"Hmm?" he answered as he thought about the pain he had caused her. She took him back after Carolina, and they had done their best to move forward. But he had never let go of the guilt.

"Domingo, who did the ambulance take?" she asked again, turning to face him. And then he heard the question and remembered the ambulance parked halfway up the plaza yesterday.

"Eva."

"Are you sure?" she asked in disbelief, placing her glasses between the first set of snap buttons of her house-coat. "Did she have the baby?" She shook her head no, answering her own question.

He had found it unusual that Celeste had not opened her terrace door. This was how they kept tabs on each other—the old folks in the neighborhood. Rosalinda went to physical therapy every Wednesday morning for a replaced hip. Drunk Esperanza circled the block at least three times every morning and then disappeared until the evening. Carmen went to eight a.m. mass every day, her metal cane announcing each step she took with a *tap-tap* on the sidewalk. Maria and Pedro went to the coffee shop around seven and had breakfast at the counter, and by now, Celeste would have opened her door. Domingo would miss the neighborhood and his friends. He saw how Elli wrinkled her nose at the closed terrace door.

Somehow, Eva, Celeste's granddaughter, had gotten mixed up with Marco, the local drug dealer. It had been clear to Domingo and just about anybody who cared to look that it was Marco's brother, Lorenzo, who worshipped the girl. But Domingo knew from his own experience that the heart could be blind, fickle, and cruel.

"Did she have the baby?" Elli asked again, looking at Domingo.

"Eh, no ... no." After a long moment, he said, "She lost it."

"Oh, no." Elli sighed.

Domingo looked into his wife's clear brown eyes and knew she was locked inside a memory. He had stood by her on that sweltering day long ago, gripping her arm tightly as she clutched her chest and tried to follow the tiny casket into the ground. He watched her now as her breath became shallow, and she seemed to fold into herself. Her eyes filled with tears, she stood up and shook her head.

"I'm sorry," he said as he stood and wrapped his arms around her. She sighed and leaned into him.

As Domingo held her, Elli noticed a thick vein that snaked across the width of his hand. She felt the sudden urge to trace it, to feel how deep and far it went. She looked up at his face and realized that his hair was almost all gray, his light brown eyes seemed smaller due to his heavy brows, and his messy unshaven white beard against his black skin made him look older than his nearly seventy years. His hands, though, were still large and strong, and in them, she could still see the young man who jumped over the back gate and sneaked into her bedroom late at night. She smiled at the thought of all those passionate embraces.

She squeezed him tighter before letting him go and went into the kitchen to finish packing. Tomorrow the movers were coming. It had taken them a long time, but they finally bought a three-family home with their eldest son, Efrain. She was excited about living with her two granddaughters — Maria Zorida, who was two, and Lilliana, who was just a few months old. She and her daughter-in-law, Jennifer, were already planning the garden. As she pushed a box into the corner, Anita, her best friend, called.

"What happened?" Elli asked immediately.

Anita took a long time to respond. Elli barely noticed the silence as she wrapped a dinner plate in newspaper.

"The baby was stillborn."

Elli shut her eyes and held onto the cardboard box tightly. "Okay," she said and hung up.

She sat down for a long while, keeping thoughts of her own baby girl, Zorida, at bay. She went downstairs to get some air, clear her head a little. She saw Manuel's pink-red, bald head as he strutted into the plaza, and she attempted to widen the space between them. If he noticed, it made no difference. He closed the gap between them in seconds with his long thin legs. Manuel was the neighborhood gossip, and he delighted in all the details of everything he saw or heard. Elli wasn't interested in the details, at least not today. She kept moving, and he stepped in right beside her.

"Oyiste?"

"Yes," Elli nodded and stopped abruptly. She turned around. Sometimes the only way to stop Manuel was either to tell him to shut up or to simply move away. Amazingly,

neither one offended him; he just moved on to the next person.
"I saw them put her in the ambulance. She was laughing, que
pena," were the last words she heard Manuel say. She left him
mid-sentence as he described the fat paramedic. As she walked
back home, she saw the usual group of boys that hung out in
front of the building. They were strangely quiet; she looked
from one face to another, and they all avoided her eyes.

"Pedroito," she called out to the one boy she knew.

Pedro walked over to her. She walked toward the door;
he hesitated and then jumped in front of her to open it.
Elli smiled, remembering when her own boys were in that
awkward stage, learning to be men. She stepped through
the first glass door of the vestibule with Pedro. Pedro
was tall and husky, working on becoming muscular. Elli
wanted to know about Lorenzo, the baby's uncle. "Where is
Lorenzo?"

"I don't know," Pedro said, frowning.

Elli asked after Marco, the baby's father.

He shrugged his shoulders.

"Eva?"

"Still in the hospital." Pedro didn't mean to say anything else, but he had not had a chance to talk to anyone —
not Lorenzo, not even his mother. "They had to keep her,"
he said quickly. "She started screaming and scratching her
belly. She scratched herself until she bled. They had to tie
her hands down." The words spilled out of him so fast he
struggled to catch his breath.

Elli grabbed his arm and then leaned against him to
comfort and quiet him. She held him gently as his body
trembled.

"Pedro," she said as she stepped back and touched his
face. He swallowed the sob that threatened to overtake him
and looked outside. He exhaled deeply and dropped his
hands, suddenly aware that he was touching her.

"Come upstairs. I'll give you some water, and you can sit
down for a minute." He stepped away from her and shook his
head.

Domingo first saw Carolina at Junior's bodega. Domingo was in the back room of the bodega about to play a number when Carolina walked in, her long white skirt trying to keep up with the impossible rhythm of her hips. She stood right in front of him as though he were not there and said, "7-0-5," and placed a twenty on the counter.

"How much?" Junior asked.

"The whole thing. I had a dream," she said as she brushed her long curly hair away from her face.

Junior smiled and said, "I love it when people have dreams," and put the twenty on top of his growing stash.

It was early morning. Domingo was dusty and sweaty in his dark blue uniform and had just played 4-1-2 because that's the time he had taken his break. He had started to make a fresh pot of coffee and noticed the white clock-face with its crisp black numbers. The clock was bright, in contrast to the drab gray and army-green room with its old plastic picnic tables and folding chairs. A calendar was tacked on to a small corkboard. It was the only decoration in the room.

As night foreman, he took his break before most of the men and women on the floor. He liked the quiet of the break room; all that could be heard was the small tick-tock of the second hand moving across the clockface. When he turned on the coffeemaker and looked up, the time seemed to leap out at him. He wrote the number down on the top right-hand corner of the schedule he was working on for the next month.

But he forgot all of that when he saw Carolina and even wished her luck as she walked past him. He wanted to follow her bangle-filled light brown wrist, her swaying hips, and her frizzy-curly hair out the door. He stood there only because he forgot how to walk.

He saw her again at Pacito's bar a month later. She sat right next to him, on the only empty stool, her hip brushed up against his as she sat down. She looked at him, smiled, ignored the man at the other end of the bar ordering, and yelled at Johnny, the bartender,   "Rum and coke." She put her bag on the bar and began digging in it. When Johnny placed the drink in front of Carolina, Domingo slid a ten toward Johnny with a nod. She turned to look at Domingo again; her eyes were sea green. Looking into them, he thought he was diving into the Caribbean Sea. He held on to the bar to steady himself. Her gaze on him was sharp and relentless as she pulled out a hair clip and gathered her wild hair into a ponytail. He turned away, feeling seasick, his face suddenly hot. He was startled when she clicked her glass against his. She smiled and took a long sip of her drink.

"Ven," she said, grabbed his hand, and pulled him to the dance floor. He held her gently, at an appropriate distance. He wanted, however, to feel the plushness of her breast against his chest; he was desperate to claim her hips with his hands and tangle his fingers in her hair. He kept himself in check. Each time he glanced into her eyes, he felt the floor shift beneath him. He looked at the top of her hair as they moved across the floor; it was the safest place on her.

He had gone to Pacito's that Saturday afternoon out of boredom. When he woke up, the apartment was quiet and empty. It usually was. The boys were off playing or practicing in all the countless activities that Elli insisted that they take part in — baseball, football, karate, swimming. Once she dropped off the boys, she and Anita had breakfast at Rudy's diner before going off to do the weekly grocery shopping and laundry. It would be at least another hour before Elli would get home. Usually, those early Saturday afternoons were their time to catch up, drink a leisurely cup of coffee, and whisper quietly in bed after sex before the boys stormed in. That Saturday, he felt restless. He got up, showered, dressed, and went out. He could see the bar from the corner and thought it might be nice to have a cold beer and watch the Yankee game.

He wasn't thinking of Elli or the boys when he spun Carolina around the dance floor. If he had been thinking, he would have stopped at that first dance. Had he been thinking, he would not have returned every Saturday with the hope of seeing her again. He would not have bought her drink after drink until she finally let him kiss her right on the dance floor. Even now, after fifteen years, with the midday sun on his face, he recalled the taste of their first kiss—salty, warm, and invigorating. He chased her with no other goal in mind than to have her. He did not think beyond that moment.

They met every Saturday for the first two months after Elli and the boys left for the day. He bounced out of bed—never mind that he worked a double and barely slept. Just the thought of her raspy voice against his ear was enough to make him sing in the shower. Remembering the feel of her hands on his chest as she said, "Wait, wait," when he jumped in bed with her was all the energy he needed. He grew excited at the thought of her lying in bed naked as he traced his tongue around her nipples, then slowly down to her navel. "Do it, Papi," she would say, her voice a husky whisper. He looked into her eyes, held onto her hips, and plunged himself into her salty wetness.

It was easy now to see how everything had gone wrong, how he had blundered and hurt his family. He tried to recall the morning he decided to head to Carolina's instead of going home and could not. Carolina had altered everything for him. With her, he longed for things he had thought no longer possible—lazy afternoons at the beach eating fried fish, playing baseball, and making sancocho in his grandmother's backyard. She made him yearn not only for his youth but for some intangible feeling, something that made him seem grand and heroic.

Carolina always had breakfast waiting for him, and he would eat as though it were his last meal, always wanting more. She would please him, shower, and then throw him out, with her scratchy voice telling him to go home, get some rest; she'd need him back on Friday or Saturday or whatever day she dictated.

The sound of a car horn from the street startled Domingo into the present. How could Carolina still mean so much to him? The truth was he couldn't unravel her from his life. He remembered the day he first saw her the same way he remembered the day he met Elli standing proudly behind the counter of her father's colmado. He remembered meeting Carolina the same way he remembered the day his infant daughter, Zorida, died, and Elli screamed and screamed until she lost her voice. He remembered Carolina's smile the way he remembered the day Efrain took his first little steps and the way Felipe came home all excited and told him about kissing a girl. He remembered everything about her. It was useless to deny her importance, and it surprised him that he still wanted to.

Domingo looked inside and noticed Elli moving about in the kitchen. Maybe their life wasn't perfect, but Elli hadn't deserved the pain he caused her. And yet, he couldn't quite regret his time with Carolina. As he watched Elli do what she had done so many times, set the dinner table, he resolved to be a better man to her, to bring her joy in a way that he probably hadn't in years.

He walked into the living room and helped her set the table—white rice, black beans, maduros, and stewed chicken. It was the last night of a homecooked meal until they got settled into their new home. She had made all his favorites. He was moved by the gesture and wanted to thank her, but he didn't know how to thank her for years of devotion, care, and love. He was struck by how much he loved her. During dinner, he dared to ask her a question he would not have thought possible earlier that morning:

"Elli, are you happy?"

After what seemed like a long silence, she said, "I'm content," and smiled at him.

Content is a good starting place, he thought and returned the smile. After dinner, as he gathered up the paper plates in one hand, he leaned down to kiss her forehead, and she stretched up, expecting it.

"Hola," Anita called as she walked in, her voice loud and cheery. Anita held a boxed cake in her hands. "This is for you," she said.

Elli held it carefully. She looked up at Anita with tears in her eyes. Tonight was different; this was their last night living across the hall from each other.

"No, no," said Anita.

The box had Anita's Dulces' label on it. In the corner of the box, Anita had written, "para mi mejor amiga."

"Ay, Anita." Elli tried to hold back the tears.

"You are only a bus trip away. We'll visit."

Elli nodded her head aggressively and brushed the tears away. She opened the box and smiled and then laughed. It was her favorite: pineapple upside-down cake. For years, Anita had been trying to teach Elli how to make it. But no matter what Anita told her to do, watched her do, Elli's cakes flattened, dropped, and burned. Anita marveled at the failure of each cake. So, on special occasions, Anita made the pineapple upside-down cake for Elli. For the past two years, since their retirements, they spent almost every evening going back and forth to each other's apartment, watching novelas, reminiscing, gossiping about the latest neighborhood happenings, having tea, and eating cake.

Elli met Anita for the first time when she went to throw the trash out one evening. The hallway smelled sweet, and Anita's door had been slightly ajar as she walked back to her apartment. This was the lady that Felipe bought slices of cake from after school. "Hola," Elli said, trying hard not to peek in as she leaned slightly forward.

"Hola," a disembodied voice said. "Un momento, Mercedes."

Elli heard footsteps and then, "Mercedes?"

"No, it's Elli, your neighbor, la mama de Felipe."

"Pero bueno, Doña, entre, entre," said Anita. "I thought you were Mercedes; she's always late picking up her cake."

Anita was gorgeous—tall, thin, and her skin pure, black perfection. Her almond eyes grew smaller as she smiled. Her cheekbones seemed sculpted, and her pouty lips were dark purple. Anita waved her in as she retied a

red scarf on her thick, kinky hair. Elli stood mesmerized for
a moment.

Anita pulled her forward. "Come in, come in." The living room was a mess of flour, dirty bowls, and bake pans.

"Excuse the regero. I'll make us tea. I just finished a
class."

"You teach?"

"Baking. Not just Dominican cakes, all kinds."

"When? How?"

"I teach twice a week. Felipe's one of my best customers," she said, raising her voice over the running water as
she filled the teakettle. "I teach on Wednesday evenings
and Saturday mornings."

"So that's what Felipe does with my hard-earned money."

"Thank you," she said and winked.

And they both laughed. And just like that, they became
inseparable. Every Sunday, Anita stopped by with a whole
chocolate cake or pound cake or Elli's soon-to-be-favorite,
a pineapple upside-down cake for the family to share. Over
time, Anita told Elli about her mother and sister in SanTíago.
She was hoping to bring them to New York in the next year
or two. All the extra money she earned she sent to her mother; the rest she saved for when they came to live with her.

Elli and Anita became like sisters. Anita hadn't realized
how lonely she had been until Elli started inviting her to
have breakfast before her Saturday class. She missed the
inside jokes, the knowing looks, the shared gossip, and even
the perceived slights of her own family. The boys made her
feel motherly. She had forgotten how messy, stinky, and
perpetually hungry boys always were; she grew up with
four brothers. She and her sister Maria Rosa would gather
in their corner of the room, hoping their brothers ignored
them as they came and went from their escapades. Anita
became an aunt to the boys, confidante to Elli, and base-
ball-watching companion to Domingo. They celebrated
Efrain's getting into college, Domingo's promotion to night
foreman, and Anita's having Ruby's diner as her first offi-
cial client.

Elli cut two thick slices of the cake. She knew Anita and she would see each other often; they'd make a point of it. They'd been through too much to let a twenty-minute bus ride get in the way. But they both knew that this, the way it was this very night, with the baseball play-by-play coming from the bedroom, the neighborhood kids playing out in the courtyard, as they sat in the dining room about to talk about Eva, would change.

"I gave my condolences to Celeste," Anita said.

Elli just nodded her head. She would go and sit with Eva when she came back home.

"To lose a child . . ." Anita started to say. "She never even got to hold her baby." She fell suddenly silent, remembering Zorida. She looked at Elli and said, "Perdóneme."

Elli's hands fluttered. "There is nothing to forgive."

Zorida had been Elli's proudest moment. She was a proper woman after marrying Domingo, but to give birth to a girl-child in her family was a triumph. She could see the pride in her mother, Martina, as they stood over Zorida's crib. They ignored little Efrain as he whimpered at their feet. They knew that Zorida would carry on their traditions. Not only would she place a plátano leaf over the white rice as it cooked, but she would make the yearly pilgrimage to Higüey with an offering to La Virgen de Altagracia. Grandmother and mother would watch to see where Zorida's talents lay: visions, dreams, la Barajas, or shells. They would guide Zorida slowly and quietly into their secret religion.

One afternoon, Elli had laid Zorida down for a nap and she never woke up. Elli barely ate, held Efrain, or even looked at Domingo. Her mother seemed to be the only one to coax words from her, but no matter how many times her mother asked, Elli would not pray, go to church, light a candle, or meet with her Spiritual Sisters. Nothing Martina said convinced her. God, the Saints, *her* Spirits had

forsaken Elli. None had warned her about Zorida. There
had been no omen, no black pebble in the rice, no suspi-
cious shell when cast, not even a stumble when she walked
through the cane fields. There had been no sign, and she
would never forgive them for that. She gave her rosary to
her sister Margarita and invited her Sisters to take what
they wanted from her altar while her mother watched and
cried. Elli removed the offerings one by one—the sweet
black coffee, the apple drizzled in honey, the black beans
and rice, the cigar and shot of rum. She threw the seawater
in the river and scattered the sand along a dirt path. As she
walked back home that day, Efrain came running toward
her and she picked him up, to their surprise. He snuggled
close to her, and she held onto him for the rest of the day.
When Domingo came home, she greeted him with a smile.

"Let's go," she said.

"Where?" he asked, as though it mattered.

"Nueva York. It's time."

He nodded yes. And then she laughed at Efrain trying
to bite off a piece of sugarcane stalk.

"Elli," Anita said, louder than she had intended to, and
reached for Elli's hand. Startled, Elli blinked several times.
They held hands for a moment. "Come on, let's get these
last boxes packed," Anita said and stood up.

They packed the last set of plates, pots, pans, and Elli's
extensive salt and pepper shaker collection. Elli brewed a
fresh pot of tea as Anita cut a second piece of cake to share.
With all the news of Eva and her baby, Anita had forgotten
to tell Elli about Carolina. She leaned in and whispered,
"Carolina..."

Elli's back immediately straightened.

Anita grabbed Elli's hand. "Carolina is dead."

Elli's eyes widened, and goose bumps suddenly appeared on her arms. "Qué?"

"This morning, el corazón. She was at Paquito's laughing at a joke Luis was telling when she placed her hand on
her chest and fell to the floor."

"Oh, Dios," Elli covered her mouth in shock.

"Will you tell him?" Anita asked.

After Anita left, Elli went to the terrace. It was unusually quiet for a warm spring night, and she fanned herself with the newspaper Domingo left on his chair. She sat on her rocking chair, her mind still a whirlwind of thoughts — Eva's baby, Zorida, and now that woman. If there had been clues before he spent the first night away from home, she failed to see them. It was easy with Domingo's schedule to lose track of time. He worked nights, and when he could, he'd pull double shifts. She slept alone most nights, and her days were filled with the boys, work, Anita, and her sister, Margarita. Domingo had become someone she saw in passing for a quick cup of coffee in the morning and rare dinners when he didn't work overtime or have to cover for someone who called in sick. She especially liked their occasional lovemaking on Saturdays. Elli wondered which came first: the woman or the drinking. However it started, it was clear that in the end, they were intertwined. She had sensed something different at first but couldn't quite put her finger on it. One Saturday afternoon she came home early from doing the laundry and grew excited when she heard him awake, humming. She smiled to herself, smoothed down her blouse, and licked her lips. She was missing him, and she hoped they could have one of their "quiet" afternoons.

She peeked into the bedroom and was surprised to see him fully dressed and splashing cologne on himself. She noticed he had on his nice blue slacks and his dress shoes. He was buttoning his short-sleeved guayabera when she stepped in and asked, "Adónde vas?"

"Mujer." He was surprised to see her standing by the door. He smiled and finished buttoning his shirt. "I'm going to Paquito's," he said as he walked quickly by her.

It took her a few days to mention it to Anita. Anita listened but said nothing. Then, one rainy afternoon, Anita walked her to the corner. They stood across the street of Paquito's bar for ten minutes, huddled silently under

Anita's little black umbrella. "Qué?" Elli asked. Anita simply nodded and looked in the direction of the bar. And then
Elli saw them. He was laughing, his arm around *her*. They
didn't have an umbrella, and they didn't care. He pulled her
even closer to him as they turned the corner.

For months, she did nothing. She argued about his
drunkenness but not about the woman. Thinking back on
it now, she cringed at her cowardice. It had taken her time,
and with the support of Anita and Margarita, she figured out
what to do. The boys were shocked when she told them she
was leaving their father. She knew they had heard the fights;
Efrain would go outside, and Felipe headed to Anita's.

"What?" Felipe said, the freckles on his cheeks darkening.

"I can't take the drinking anymore."

Efrain stared at her.

"Mami, what about us?" Felipe said, his eyes brimming
with tears. She grabbed and held him tight against her. She
explained that she was sending them to their uncle Eduar-
do in Santo Domingo for the summer. She would find them
an apartment while they were away.

"I'm not leaving," Efrain mumbled as he stood. His tall
thin frame casting a shadow over them

"Ay, Efrain, por favor," she pleaded.

Efrain refused. His eyes unblinking, his dark face hard
and arms crossed. He knew what his mother would not say;
he had seen them together, his father and that woman.

"Efrain!" she yelled.

"I'm not leaving you." Then he quickly corrected himself. "I'm not leaving." And besides, he already had a summer job, he said, and he wasn't going to give it up.

"Okay, okay, Efrain," she said.

Remembering the night she confronted Domingo still made
her anxious. Felipe was safely in Santo Domingo, and
Efrain was at her sister's house. She waited up all night for
Domingo. She fortified herself with coffee and listened for

the key in the lock. When he stumbled in, she said, "Viejo."

"I'll stop. I promise to stop drinking," he said, thinking he knew what she was about to say.

"Drink all you want."

He blinked slowly as her words sunk in.

She gave him no time to recover. "That woman, Caro—" she started to say her name and then stopped herself. No wife should have to say the name of her husband's mistress. She sighed. Her logic seemed silly, immature, but at that moment, it was all she had. She held back the tears and said, "You have to stop seeing that woman." She stood right in front of him and smelled the rum on his breath. "Viejo," her voice cracked a little, and she stopped herself.

"Mujer, what are you talking about?"

"It must end, or I will go."

Her words cleared his mind, and, looking directly at her, he said, "You won't leave."

She walked away, swatting the air with her hand, picked up her already-packed bag, and left. She remembered how his eyes widened as she turned away. She never asked him what he did that night. Did he look for the boys? Did he search the apartment for their things? Or did he go back to *her*?

After the first week of being in an empty apartment, Domingo went to see her. "Come back home." There were only two places Elli would go—Anita's, who lived across the hall, or Margarita's, three blocks away on Intervale. He headed to Margarita's.

"Why?" She held the door slightly open.

"It's where you belong." He tried to push the door, but she was stronger than she looked and held the door firmly in place.

"And what about her?" She gave him a long look through the thin gap in the door. His face looked gaunt, his eyes puffy, and he kept shifting his weight from foot to foot.

"I can stop everything."

"Prove it to me," she said as she closed the door. She forced herself to turn the lock; she pressed her hand against

the door as though the deadbolt were not enough to keep
her from reaching out to him. When she heard his footsteps
going down the stairs, she walked back to her sister, fell
into her arms, and sobbed.

Domingo came back to see Elli a month later. "Come
home, Elli." And before she could ask why, he said, "Te
necesito."

She looked at him hard; he was still thin but more
himself. She closed the door softly without answering.

That summer, Efrain worked his first summer job, and
Anita came to see her almost every night. When Elli and
Margarita stood next to each other, Margarita looked like
a sharper image of Elli. Margarita was lighter, no freckles, her hair was thick and lush, and she kept it clipped in
a loose ponytail. Her fingers were long, thin, and delicate
looking, and she was thin and petite. Elli's hair was short
and not quite straight or curly, her nose broader, full of
freckles as though they found their favorite spot and gathered there. Her nails were clean and long, but her hands
looked as though they knew hard work. And she was on the
verge of plumpness.

Anita reported if she had seen Domingo. They often saw
each other. Sometimes he would say, as he walked past her
on the way home with a bag of takeout, "Tell her I miss her
and the boys," and Anita would nod.

Elli went to see him on a Saturday, she remembered.
They stared at each other when she walked in. He was in
the kitchen looking groggy as he put the greca on the stove.
He was barefoot and wore a wrinkled white t-shirt and blue
shorts.

His hands shook as he turned on the burner.

She had a speech prepared, but she couldn't remember
a single word.

"Are you coming home? I stopped drinking," he said.
She waited for the rest.

"It's all over."

Her shoulders sagged for a second, and then she

straightened up. She looked him in the eyes.

"Te lo huro," he said, sensing her doubt.

She listened to his promise, still standing by the door with her keys in her hands. And nodded yes.

Domingo only half-listened to the baseball play-by-play coming from his small radio. He thought about the day he said to Carolina, "No más." He stood by her front door, tempted to go farther but knew he'd simply better not. As much as Carolina excited him, he loved his family and felt stupid that he had ever thought that Carolina was the woman for him. She had always been very clear with him. "Amorsito," she would say, "you know, this is all I want. I want you on Saturdays, sometimes Fridays, on occasion the whole weekend, if your life allows for that. I'm not interested in your other life. I'm only interested in you when you are here. You understand?"

"Sí, sí," he would answer hurriedly as he kissed her neck, breasts, hips, and thighs. She shook her head.

Domingo thought he was different, different from the previous men in Carolina's life, when he saw the brand new greca, still in the box, one Saturday morning. Yes, she had bought the stovetop espresso maker for him, she answered matter-of-factly. Since she was looking away, she did not see the excitement in his eyes. "You always complain about the coffee from the bakery. I figured I'd save you time and the both of us the complaint. And you can make it yourself. Bought you some coffee too; it's in the fridge. That's what it said on the can. 'Keep refrigerated.'" He stared at her behind as she placed the rest of the groceries away with that lovesick look on his face.

When he stood by her door, refusing to step farther in, and looked into her eyes, she sighed and nodded knowingly. "I've always liked the look of her."

"What?" he said incredulously.

Carolina shrugged her shoulders, speaking mostly to

herself, "If I were different, I might have tried to be her friend."

In his stupor to be around Carolina, it had never occurred to him that Elli and Carolina had seen each other.

Domingo didn't like the sound of Elli's name coming out of Carolina's mouth. He wanted to make her stop, smack her, but he couldn't move, couldn't breathe.

"Go home. We both know she deserves better."

She was dead, Elli whispered. A sob so loud escaped her that she scared herself. Carolina embodied a woman on the move for Elli. Her body was fluid, shapely, her hair was always piled high in a mass of loose curls, her mouth was serious, but her light eyes seemed playful, and the one time Elli heard her laugh, Elli couldn't resist, she turned to look at her. It had been close to fifteen years, maybe more. His affair had been a stain on their relationship, but it couldn't be all there was. They were good before *her*, and they were all right after.

Eli refilled the greca and put it on the stove. It was unusual for her to make coffee so late at night, but she needed a cafecito to strengthen her. It was time they finally moved past that woman.

"Domingo," she said as she walked into the bedroom.

He glanced at her, the sweet scent of coffee coming off her.

She walked toward him, stared into his small eyes, and reached out for him. She grabbed both his hands. He looked at her, confused, held her hands, and stood without understanding why. "Are you okay?"

She nodded yes and leaned in close, their bodies only inches away from each other, and for the first time, she spoke Carolina's name to him.

His body started to fall back, but she held him; *her* grip was strong and tight.

Lorenzo

Lorenzo stumbles home around three in the morning. He removes his Timbs by the door and heads quietly to his bedroom. His hand reaches for it before he even knows what he is doing. He opens the top drawer of his dresser. On the left are his neatly folded white t-shirts; on the right are his special things. There is a picture of his father, brother, and him when he was little. His older brother Marco faces away from the camera. His father, in the middle, looks straight ahead, smiling brilliantly. Beside the picture is a small round jewelry box that belonged to his mother. In it are two precious things: his father's watch and a faded pink barrette.

He reaches for the pink barrette.

The barrette strips his mind clean. All of his loneliness and misdeeds disappear. The clean white space centers him. He lays down on his bed. He doesn't bother to take off his clothes. He is anxious to see her face and imagine her hand in his. It starts the same way; he can't rush the memory, or the dreaming won't work. He closes his hand around the barrette and then his eyes. And like magic, she appears.

They were thirteen, walking home from school. Eva was with the twins, Maribel and Marisol. Her thick curly hair was in two long braids held by pink barrettes at the ends. Her braids swayed gently against her denim jacket.

Lorenzo and Pedro walked a few feet behind them. Lorenzo had not yet built up the nerve to speak to her. He felt Pedro's big hand slap him on the back and propel him forward. He bumped into and almost fell on her. His heart almost stopped when she turned around and looked at him.

"Hi Lorenzo," she said as she helped steady him.

"Hi," he said, his face red, his throat dry as he stood up, holding the barrette that had fallen off her braid. He was distracted by her warm hand on his arm, and he forgot about the barrette. Pedro suggested to the twins that they should head for the bodega. Lorenzo found himself walking side by side with Eva. He slipped the barrette absent-mindedly into his pocket.

He smiles at the memory. He can never remember if he said anything to her at that moment. What he does remember is how they walked into the grocery store and she got chocolate cupcakes and he got Twinkies. Before she put her fifty cents on the counter, he paid for both. She smiled and said, "Thank you." He felt tall and smart.

The memory is the gateway to daydreaming about Eva. For years he has created fantasies of the two of them, holding hands, kissing, laughing, and once he has had sex, of seeing Eva in ecstasy from his touch. It is like an elaborate music video that he could rewind as often as he needs to.

Tonight, more than ever, he wants to disappear, to forget, to see only Eva's smiling face. He feels tired, broken. He desperately wants to drift to sleep to her sweet face. But the barrette is not working. Instead, he relives the moment with his girlfriend, Tonya, endlessly. Tonya's face and sharp words make him restless. His whole body starts to itch. He sees Tonya's face streaked with tears. Her eyes are downcast, her hand holding the edge of her white dresser dotted with splattered paint drops. It does not matter that he squeezes the barrette so tight it leaves an imprint in the center of his palm.

Around five in the morning, the image of Tonya's glare begins to fade, and the feeling that he has failed at something crucial dissipates. The irritation on his skin subsides.

Finally, he thinks, sleep will come; he turns on his side, and the gray-blue light filters through the blinds, slicing the floor into neatly stacked rectangles.

Later that morning, Lorenzo gets up, showers, and dresses. He needs time to think of what he was going to say to Tonya. He puts the barrette back in his mother's jewelry box. He is still hopeful. He does not yet realize that last night was the end. He slips his wallet into the back of his Levi's, puts on a fresh, crisp, oversized white t-shirt over his sleeveless one, and settles for his Jordans instead of the Timbs. He glances at his outfit in the mirror, notices his red and puffy eyes, and pulls his Yankee cap low over his overgrown floppy hair. He walks by Tía's bedroom and hears her slow, melodic praying as he checks his beeper and walks out.

He wishes the weather matched his mood: overcast and chilly. But the sky is clear, and the heat of the sun presses on him with its bright cheeriness. He heads for Josefina's Bakery, buys an overly sweet coffee, pan caliente, *The Daily News*, and sits by the basketball courts. Someone cruising by blasts Method Man and Mary J. Blige's "You're All I Need."

Even when the skies were gray,
You would rub me on my back and say, "Baby it'll be okay."

Immediately, Lorenzo sees Tonya's sweet face, remembers her soft hands on him, her smile, and then last night's tears. Hot coffee spills onto his hand. "Shit," he says as he shakes off the coffee and tries to shake off last night's memories of Tonya. Mary J. Blige's melody fades as the car moved on:

I'll dedicate my life...

He looks down at the paper and sees the Yankees' new shortstop Derek Jeter's jaw-dropping jump-throw. As he pulls the paper closer to read about it, he hears the quick whoop whoop of what sounds like a siren, and his chest tightens.

Where was Marco?

He closes his eyes and remembers that it had been a while since he was his brother's lookout. These days, they are their own men. They keep their distance from each other. Lorenzo glances up. It is only an ambulance. If Marco knew he confused the sounds, he'd call him soft, a pussy. Lorenzo spits a big wad and whispers, "Fuck you."

He stares up and down the block and watches as yet another car misses the "Dead End" sign and rides up the street. It gets caught in the circular loop that anchors the center of the block. The neighborhood is round enough to feel womblike and comforting. Today, Lorenzo feels trapped and confined. Today, he wants out.

He sips what is left of his coffee and remembers how his father, Gabriel, always let him have a taste of his when he was little. The memory makes him both happy and sad. Lorenzo remembers how handsome his father was. He had a dark rich complexion, silky black hair, deep-set black eyes, a long elegant nose, and thin lips that hid behind an overgrown goatee. Everybody called him by his nickname, Indio.

The first few months after their father died, Lorenzo and Marco worried that they would be taken away from Tía. She assured them, with her small fist hitting her chest, that no one would take her boys from her. When the courts finally decided to give custody of both him and Marco to Tía instead of their maternal grandparents, they were all relieved. Tía kissed the custody papers and placed them next to a picture of his father. In the photo, his father's clothes are dirty, his eyes red and small from a long night of work, but his smile is wide and bright as he looks into the camera. They celebrated that night.

Tía Flores invited the family court lawyer, Joseph Dorhout, over to dinner. Much to their surprise, not only did he come, but he also brought his wife, Lisa. Tía went all out. There was arroz con pollo, black beans, spicy green beans and onions, maduros, arepes de yuca and, to top it off, Tía made her famous coconut cake. Joseph said he wished all his clients were like Tía, feisty. Tía just laughed and then said matter-of-factly that she told the judge the truth, that Juan and Celia, the boys' grandparents, have not seen the boys in years, and that they had disowned their only daughter, the boys' mother, Maria. Tía whispered to no one in particular that she believed Juan and Celia were after Indio's pension and life insurance benefits.

Once Lorenzo knew that he was safe with Tía, he finally let himself grieve. He was thirteen, almost a man, his father said, a couple of days before he died of a massive heart attack. And still, Lorenzo cried like a baby. He couldn't help it; the ache was deep in his chest. He often went to his room after school and cried himself to sleep. Sometimes he felt Tía's warm hands on his back. She never shushed him or told him it is going to be all right; she just let him cry and be sad.

The sudden and loud arguments between Tía and Marco brought Lorenzo out of his grief. Tía Flores yelling, "Marco Antoñio deja esa mierda."

And Marco yelling back, "I don't know what you're talking about."

Tía is the kind of person who believes in having the last word.

"Stop lying to me. And don't bring that shit in my house."

Marco sighed and turned his back to her.

"What's going on?" Lorenzo asked one afternoon.

Marco sucked his teeth. "Same shit."

Lorenzo shrugged his shoulders, unsure of what to say or what that meant. Marco emptied his pockets of several dime bags. Lorenzo's eyes widened. "What's that?"

"What do you think?"

Lorenzo took a good look at his brother. Marco was handsome. He had their mother's thick curly hair and hazel eyes. Lorenzo imagined that, depending on Marco's mood, his eyes could look either menacing or inviting. Marco also inherited his mother's small, thick stature, which made him stocky. He had, however, their father's caramel complexion and smile. Like his father's, Marco's smile was beautiful.

When the arguing got loud between Tía and Marco, he grabbed one of Tía's CDs and popped it into his Sony Discman. There were stacks of CDs everywhere in their small apartment. If Tía wasn't praying, she was singing the latest Latin hit. He just grabbed whatever looked interesting. For Lorenzo, it was less about the music and more about drowning out their voices. And it worked — he disappeared into the music.

At first, before the barrette, when he listened to merengue, he tried conjuring up images of his parents. But the only image he had of the two of them is their wedding picture. Maria looked straight at the camera with a ready laugh. She wore a pink dress and had a small bouquet of daffodils. His father is in a navy-blue suit, white shirt, and white and blue striped tie that is loosened. He had eyes only for his new wife, his smile wide and bright. What Lorenzo remembers is when Tía would wave his father over, and they danced across the living room, hips swaying, with smiles on both their faces.

Once he has the barrette, Eva slips into all his fantasies.

One day Marco stayed out almost all night, so when Tía woke him up to go to school, he was angry. He yelled, and she yelled right back that he has to go to school or go to work.

He threw a bunch of twenties in her face. Tía stared at Marco until he looked away, and she gathered up all the money as calmly as she could, although Lorenzo could see her hands shaking. She folded them up and put them on Marco's dresser. "Take your dirty money and get out, and don't come back unless you decide to do right by us and your father's memory." Marco looked at her like he didn't understand what she is saying.

"Pack," she said, "or I will throw all your things out."

For a second, Lorenzo thought Marco was going to cry, but then his face hardened, his lips pressed together tightly as he took his things and threw them in garbage bags.

For weeks afterward, Tía saved Marco's dinner plate in the microwave. Each morning after, she threw it away, but not before praying out loud that the Lord please protect her baby. Both Tía and Lorenzo asked Marco's friends if they knew where he was, if he was okay. "Tell him," Tía said, "that we miss him." They shrugged their shoulders and walked away. Tía sighed. One day, Iggy, one of Marco's friends, called out to Lorenzo by the basketball court.

"Lolo?"

Lorenzo froze. Only his family called him Lolo. As he turned to follow the voice, he hoped it was Marco, but the voice was all wrong; it was too high and thin. Lorenzo squinted at Iggy and said, "Do I know you?"

"You Marco's little brother, right?" Iggy was short, small, and skinny. He was dressed in black. He had on black jeans, a black sweatshirt, and the one exception, black and white Air Jordans X.

At the mention of Marco's name, he took quick steps toward Iggy.

"Marco is living on Banana Kelly. Your aunt, she looks so sad…" Iggy took quick steps backward.

"What? Where?" He rushed up to Iggy, who just kept moving backward.

"He's with Sonia."

"I don't know Sonia," Lorenzo said.

"She's in the yellow building on the second floor," Iggy said and turned around and walked off.

"Thanks." It was good to know Marco was okay. He almost told Tía but thought better of it. He went alone and hoped he could bring Marco home.

There were three buildings on Banana Kelly that can be called yellow, sort of. The first building on the block was the brightest. The others, he decided, were just beige, but if the first building proved to be fruitless, he would try the other two. The front door lock of the building was busted, so he just walked right in. He climbed the short flight to the second floor slowly, his heart is beating fast, and his palms

sweaty. There were four apartments on the floor, two to the
left and two to the right. He stood in the hallway for a long
time, trying to decide which way to go.

When he heard someone coming slowly down the
stairs, he knew he had to decide; he couldn't just stand
there like some creepy guy. He went left and knocked on
the first door quickly before he lost his nerve. He heard a
soft scraping sound, and then the lock turned. An old man
opened the door just a little. He wore a white guayabera
with black pants and thick white socks encased in black
slippers. In his free hand, he held *El Diario*. The smell of
onions and garlic escaped from the apartment. Lorenzo
knew immediately he had made a mistake. "I'm sorry," he
said, "I was looking for Sonia."

"Sonia! Sonia! La hija de puta," the old man said in a
surprisingly loud voice.

Lorenzo backed away as the old man slammed his
door. Lorenzo headed for the stairs. He started making
excuses; maybe this was the wrong building. He would
never find Marco. He stopped when he hears the familiar beat of "The Flava in Ya Ear" remix coming from the
other end of the hallway. He took a chance that Marco was
there. He knocked on the door, and then again harder to
be heard over the music. The door opened wide, and a girl
stood there.

"Yeah?" she said. She wore frayed jean shorts and a
Stevenson High School t-shirt. Her hair was long, down
to her butt, and bone straight. "Well," she said, arching an
eyebrow.

"Marco, is he here?"

"What?" she said.

"Marco," he said louder, thankful for the lull in the
song between Biggie and Craig Mack.

She closed the door without a word. He stood there,
unsure if he should stay or go. He was about to head toward
the stairs when he saw the door open again. He smiled at
Marco, who looked groggy from sleep, and moved forward
to hug him, but Marco pulled the door close to him and

stepped forward a bit, leaving only a small gap. "What?"

Lorenzo was taken aback by Marco's behavior. He had assumed that Marco missed being home as much as he and Tía missed him. "I miss you," Lorenzo said.

Marco looked down at Lorenzo's scuffed black Converse.

When it was clear that Marco wasn't going to move or say anything, Lorenzo headed for the stairs, heartbroken.

"Hey," Marco finally said. "Let me give you money for some sneakers."

Standing by the top step, Lorenzo looked at him for a long time: Marco in the hallway, in basketball shorts, shirtless, and barefoot. Lorenzo took the stairs down, two at a time.

The next time the brothers saw each other, a few months later, Marco had a box of Jordan sneakers and a small roll of money. "Give this to Tía." Marco extended his hand with the cash.

"*You* give it to Tía."

This is how it went between the two of them. Marco showed up with a box of sneakers and money, and Lorenzo turned him down. Marco waited for him one day in front of the building. Lorenzo intended to walk by him, as usual. "Yo, man, I'm sorry."

Lorenzo stopped and looked down at him; he was a full head taller than Marco. Marco held out the bag. "No," Lorenzo said. Marco exhaled loudly. "We missed you, ya know. We worry about you."

"I know." Marco's voice was low. "Come on; let's get a bite at the diner." Marco saw the hesitation in Lorenzo, "Come on, Lolo, just you and me."

Little by little, Marco won Lorenzo over, and soon enough, Lorenzo was wearing the latest Jordans and pocketing the money. Over the next few months, Marco sweet talked Lorenzo into being his lookout with promises of continued togetherness. He said he needed someone he could trust. Lorenzo was careful, not wanting Tía to find out. She would do more than yell at him and kick him out; he was sure of that.

He finally agreed. He stood out on hot days, windy days, and cold and rainy days when there were few buyers. He learned the special short-long-short whistle to let the whole crew know the cops were rolling up. He learned the hand signals for the new and sketchy-looking buyers that were turned away the first few times. All of this just to be near Marco. Most times, Marco was on the far end of the block, watching everything that happened, and giving the go-ahead to Iggy to collect the money, while Chico delivered the product.

At first, Marco lavished praise on Lorenzo, but as it became more routine, Marco treated him just like the others — a nod greeting, directions on where to stand and to stay alert. He wasn't paying him, Marco said, to daydream. Iggy didn't move fast enough and was short fifty dollars; what did Iggy think? That he hadn't noticed? Pedro and Chico were told to stop forgetting the extra bags that stayed in their pockets when they were done for the night.

Marco made the rounds on a drizzling gray day. Lorenzo watched him walk toward him. Marco's swagger was for a man twice his size. His chest was broad, muscular, and led the way. Every step was sure and sound. People walking by could not help but stare at how handsome he was, but they also created a lot of space between him and them. It was as though they could feel his volatile energy.

He looked away and saw the old church ladies returning from afternoon mass with their heads covered in colorful scarves or black lace, the transit workers doing their never-ending work while telling dirty jokes, and the old men drinking beers a little too early in the day underneath the bodega's awning. This was not what he wanted. He was frustrated and feeling no closer to his brother. And at almost eighteen, this was not how Lorenzo wanted to spend his time. "I quit," Lorenzo said, surprising even himself.

"Yeah, nobody else is coming out in this," Marco said as he came toward Lorenzo. He dug in his pocket and took out a money clip. As he was about to hand Lorenzo some cash, Lorenzo said, "I mean for good."

"Lolo, what are you talking about?" His voice took on that dark, seductive quality.

"Don't call me Lolo."

They stared at each other.

Lorenzo wanted to wrestle on the living room floor again, watch karate movies on Saturday afternoon, and play video games for hours. He wanted his little big brother, not whoever this was.

Lorenzo hates when his memories ambush him. He looks up and sees a gurney being wheeled toward the ambulance by a husky EMT; he notices the long ponytail of tight curls hanging from it but can't make out the girl's face. Something about the girl seems familiar. He stands up to get a better look and sees Eva. He throws the coffee cup on the ground and runs to her. Eva's pretty brown face is strained and moist with sweat.

"Eva."

She smiles and extends her hand. He quickly reaches for it. Her almond-shaped brown eyes seem to shine from the pain and excitement of being in labor.

"Call . . . call Marco," she says in between short breaths. He nods. Her long curly hair is tied up in a messy ponytail, a white t-shirt clings to her chest with sweat, her old gray high school gym shorts ride low on her waist, and one of her pink chinelas hangs precariously from her big toe. Her belly is large and round, and she holds it with her other hand.

The EMT tells Eva, "Breathe, breathe, don't push yet." Eva tries to smile in between panting. Lorenzo is about to step into the ambulance when the big guy puts his hand up.

"Who are you?"

"The uncle," Lorenzo says proudly as he tries to step around the big EMT.

"The what?"

Maybe he thinks Lorenzo means Eva's uncle. He looks from Eva to Lorenzo and is about to say something when Eva shrieks and tries to sit up on the gurney.

"Get in," he says to Lorenzo and yells, "Let's go," to his partner.

Eva lays back down and closes her eyes for a few moments. "Call Marco," she says again as the technician takes her blood pressure and listens for the baby.

"Yeah, as soon as we get to the hospital."

Lorenzo stares at Eva and reaches for her hand. Her grip tightens as a contraction comes on. He watches as her face strains then relaxes. Being this close to her is better than any dream. He begins making a mental list of everything. He wants to remember everything—the day and time. It's Wednesday, May 23, 11:35 a.m. The sky is a perfect blue. It's a perfect spring day. Her forehead is beaded with sweat. The feel of her hand in his is electric. It makes him nervous and bold. He leans down and kisses her lightly on the lips. Her eyes open wide. He blushes. Eva takes her hand away and tries to sit up. The EMT gently lays her back down.

As soon as they wheel Eva through the double doors of the maternity ward, he goes over to the phone and beeps Marco, Pedro, and then calls Tía. Although he is alone among clusters of families, he feels happy, elated as he paces the long mustard-colored corridor. The families, aunts, uncles, cousins, grandparents all keep glancing nervously toward the two swinging doors at the end of the hall. Every now and then, a nurse or a beaming dad in scrubs comes out and calls out a name, and a family pops out of their seats, full of excitement.

When Pedro beeps him, he practically leaps to the telephone by the window to call him back. "I haven't seen him," Pedro says when Lorenzo asks about Marco. Lorenzo sighs. He wants someone to come to the hospital, sit with, pace, and be happy with him. Pedro says he will beep again when he finds Marco.

Lorenzo walks to the window, rubs his face, and brushes his hair back from his face. He is nervous, excited, scared. He wants to call Tonya. She would smooth his hair, kiss his neck, make him feel calm and somehow in control.

Last night, Tonya gave him that look again. "What," he said. It was more than a week since he last saw her. He could tell she was angry with him, but he didn't know why. When they saw each other, she had a barrage of questions: *Where were you? What were you doing? With whom? Why?* He responded the same way every time, "T, you know everything I do."

He complained to Pedro about Tonya's sudden change. "That's cause you're an ass," Pedro responded.

Lorenzo sucked his teeth, feeling, as usual, misunderstood by Pedro.

Tonya's look was penetrating. It made him uncomfortable. It was as though she were trying to see inside him.

He looked at the newly added details to the neighborhood mural she drew on her closet door. Some lines were darkened, and others removed. The basketball court was gone. When he turned to ask her about the court, she was giving him that look.

"What?" he said again.

She shrugged and turned to gather up her pencils.

He remembered the first time he noticed Tonya looking at him this way. A few weeks back, Eva stopped to chat with the whole crew and Tonya. They were hanging out by the basketball courts. Tonya was sketching the crack in the sidewalk in her small pad. Eva's belly was making her walk slowly. Iggy ran up to her and mimicked her walk beside her, making them all laugh.

He simply stared at her.

Pedro made her sit down on the cement benches beside Tonya, and they all hovered around. Lorenzo stood just a few steps back, looking at her. He watched intently at the way Eva rested her hands on thighs, laughed at Iggy's jokes, and how she let Tonya touch her belly. He was already recreating the scene, except it was his hand on Eva's belly. It was only when Pedro bumped him while laughing that Lorenzo came out of his daydream. He caught the sideways look that Pedro gave him in Tonya's direction. He smiled and joined the others and noticed the strange look Tonya gave him. Her eyes intense, her head with a slight tilt to the right, as she bit her bottom lip. She was giving him the same look as she gathered her pencils. "I don't want to be with you anymore," she said.

Lorenzo stared at her.

She puts the pencils in an old Bustelo can by her dresser. She took a deep breath—"I want to break up"—and then exhaled.

He was stunned. "What … why?" he finally asked. He didn't wait for her to answer. "I take you out, buy you things," he looked at the pencils, then back at her, "things that are important to you, not just teddy bears and shit. I like you. We're good together." He took a step toward her, and she stepped back.

"I like you too." She looked down at her hands, stained with graphite from the pencils.

"We're good together." His voice was soft as he took another step in her direction. He was encouraged when she didn't move away.

She looked up at him, her eyes brimming with tears. She let him take her hands in his. "I see the way you look at Eva."

He dropped her hands immediately and stepped back. "What … what." His face could not settle on an expression. His eyes widened, then narrowed, his face reddened, then paled, and finally, he frowned.

"You love her," she said, looking at him.

He stumbled backward. Eva's face flashed before him. "Please leave."

"But …"

"Just go."

He swallowed. "Eva is Marco's girl."

"I know. Do you?" The tears fell down her cheeks and she wiped them quickly away and opened the door.

Lorenzo is the last person in the waiting room. He keeps his eyes fixed on the double doors and tries not to think about how much he has hurt Tonya. Nor is he ready to admit how much and for how long he has loved Eva. When the nurse comes through the double doors, he stands instantly. It is all about the baby now.

"Are you with Eva?"

"Yes." His heart beats fast.

"Come with me."

He follows the nurse to the doors.

"Hold on just a minute; the doctor will be right out." The nurse slips back through the swinging doors as he waits again. He looks through the thick window in the door, but all he sees is a nurse's station. He steps back when he sees a man in scrubs walking toward him.

"Are you with Eva Alemán?"

"Yes."

Maybe it's a girl. Eva wants to be surprised.

"I'm Doctor Juarez. Who are you to Eva?"

"Nobody. I mean, I'm the uncle."

The doctor scrunches his brow.

"I'm the baby's uncle."

"Oh." The doctor takes off his gold-rimmed glasses and stretches out his arm to lead Lorenzo into the corner.

"I'm sorry, but the baby was stillborn. There is nothing we could have done."

Lorenzo looks into the doctor's eyes. "Stillborn?"

"The baby died in the womb."

The pain shoots through him like a bolt of lightning. "Oh God, oh God, oh God." Lorenzo leans against the wall.

"I'm sorry," the doctor says, reaching out to touch Lorenzo but not quite doing it.

"Eva?" Lorenzo asks, his voice a soft whisper.

"She will be okay."

Lorenzo sits and waits. He finds that he still wants to kiss and touch Eva. And more than anything, he wants the baby to be his, not Marco's. He is the one in love with Eva, not Marco. His skin prickles and breaks out into a sweat. He stands, rubs his thighs, and then sits back down. All of it is right there for him to see. He forces himself to remember.

He recalls how it was he who dared Marco, in front of

the whole crew—Pedro, Chico, and Iggy—that he couldn't
get the next girl that came on the block. Marco was boast-
ing about the three girls he was seeing. Lorenzo wanted
him to just shut up. It was good to be around the guys,
catching up on the jokes and gossip. For a little while, it
even felt good to be around Marco. When Marco began
to brag about all the things he was doing and talked over
everyone, Lorenzo was furious.

"You all that, make the next girl that comes on the
block yours." He just wanted Marco to shut up.

Marco smiled and shrugged his shoulders.

They were on the roundabout opposite the bodega,
scanning the block for girls. All of them quiet. Lorenzo
did not see Eva walk in and out of the bodega. It was Iggy
who saw her and called out her name. Before Lorenzo
could stop him, Marco sauntered in her direction. Lorenzo
watched in shock as Marco gently took her bags from her
and walked her to her building. The last thing Lorenzo saw
before they stepped into the building was her big smile and
Marco's wink as he looked back at them.

For a while after that, Lorenzo stopped hanging out.
Finally, Pedro bribed Tía with a thick slice of Doña Anita's
chocolate cake to let him into Lorenzo's room.

"What?" Lorenzo said when he saw Pedro standing in
the corner, seeming to take up half his room.

"They're together."

Lorenzo's face paled. Pedro watched Lorenzo until he
nodded slightly. When Lorenzo finally looked up, Pedro
was gone, and his room had reshaped itself.

It was at that moment, Lorenzo began to dream, fanta-
size, and in no time create the perfect situation. He antici-
pated the moment that he could step in as Eva's lover. The
overhead loudspeaker announcing a code-blue startles him
from his reverie. He stands and walks to the window facing
the parking lot. He sees his reflection. His skin feels like it's
sizzling under a hot sun. In his hallucination, his brother is
dead so that he can freely love a girl he barely has the courage to speak to. Does Eva even know how much he loves

her? He feels nauseous. He sits back down, bending over, and breathing heavily.

When Marco finally walks into the waiting room, his smile is so wide, Lorenzo sees his father's face and almost doesn't recognize him. Marco has an unlit cigar in one hand and a still-wrapped one in his other. It is one long, excruciating movement to stand and face his brother.

"Where is Eva? Is it a boy or a girl?" Marco slaps Lorenzo on the shoulder and then hugs him. He shoves the plastic-wrapped cigar into Lorenzo's hand. Lorenzo doesn't know how to start and instinctively leads his big brother to the same corner the doctor had led him.

"Where is Eva?"

"Marco."

"Is it a boy?"

"Marco," Lorenzo's voice is barely above a whisper.

"Yeah?" His smile is still big.

"The ba … baby…"

"Yeah?"

"It died."

Marco's face grows still. His smile freezes and then slowly melts from his face.

"The baby … was born dead."

Marco stares off into the distance, and then he doubles over, his breath coming quick and shallow. Lorenzo bends down and softly places a hand on Marco's shoulder. They remain like that for a moment, looking as though they are in prayer—Marco down on one knee, Lorenzo on his haunches.

Marco stands quickly, shaking off Lorenzo's arm from his shoulder, presses his hand on the wall to steady himself, opens his mouth to say something, turns, and walks away. His crushed cigar is scattered on the dirty linoleum floor.

Marco walks through double doors and heads directly to the nurses' station. Lorenzo follows, afraid of what Marco might do. Marco smacks into the nurses' station and says, "I need to speak to a doctor." Lorenzo is relieved. Lorenzo watches as Marco closes his eyes and grips onto the edge of the nurses' station.

"What is the patient's name?"

Marco slumps a little, "I ... I don't know my baby's name." Marco sways for a moment, and Lorenzo stands closely behind him.

The nurse looks up, her smooth dark skin crinkles around the eyes as she looks at Marco. She stares at him for so long that the tears fall down Marco's cheek. Lorenzo is shocked at Marco's tears and stands closer to him, putting his hand on Marco's shoulder again. She recognizes Lorenzo and realizes Marco must be the baby's father. Her voice low and soft, from years of practice, "Wait, one moment. I'll bring the doctor." She disappears for what seems like an eternity. She brings back a lean, tall man with glasses.

Marco looks at him, unable to speak.

"Doctor Juarez, this is the baby's father," says the nurse.

Marco nods and closes his eyes again. He wants to hear that Lorenzo lied. He wants to hear that his baby is alive and well. Something about how the doctor stands straight, frowns, and removes his glasses lets him know that Lorenzo told the truth. The doctor, still new at doctoring, looks at the nurse, and she gives him an encouraging nod.

"The baby is stillborn."

Marco opens his mouth as though to say something, and still, the words do not come.

"We don't know why these things happen."

"E ... Eva," Marco manages to say.

"Eva is okay."

Marco looks at Lorenzo, openly crying. Lorenzo hugs him tightly and then realizes Marco is sliding through his arms and onto the floor. When Marco comes to, Lorenzo, the doctor, and nurse are holding him up. They sit him down in the nurses' chair. She hurries to get him water.

"Are you okay?" asks Lorenzo.

He says yes, but nods no. He takes the cup of water from the nurse. His hand shakes as he drinks.

The nurse asks Marco, "Would you like to see him?"

"Yes," he says, his voice hoarse. He wipes his eyes

and looks down at his hand, barely understanding why his hands are wet.

The nurse tells the doctor something in a quiet voice. Lorenzo starts to walk behind Marco, but the nurse stops him. Lorenzo watches as Marco uses the wall for support as he follows the doctor.

Lorenzo watches Marco step into the room. He watches as the door closes slowly. His skin is on fire. It prickles and burns. He rubs his arms vigorously. Watching his brother break down makes Lorenzo realize how little he actually knows Marco. Just a few hours ago, he wanted to replace Marco in Eva and the baby's life. Now, he cannot stand himself. He leaves, unable to face Marco. He knows he needs to tell Marco he is sorry—for everything, but especially for hating him.

Una Ves Mas

Jorge walked onto the terrace and saw the neighborhood boys below. Most days, he enjoyed their banter, their game playing, and their eagerness to outdo each other. He watched those boys a million times and just as often imagined his own, playing, laughing, and looking up at him every once in a while. Today, he wanted the boys to shut up, for those thoughts to go away, for the day to start again, with no Eva, no baby.

When Matilde rushed in, he was enjoying the rich smell of the spicy puttanesca sauce he had just made. Matty ran to the bathroom, the bag of groceries and its contents scattered along the hallway. IniTíally, he didn't think anything of it. She often rushed and called out loudly, "I have to pee," while slamming the bathroom door shut. But as he picked up the pot to fill it with water for the pasta, he thought he heard her moan. He turned off the water, listened, and heard a loud sob. He sat the pot on the counter. "Matty." When she didn't respond, he walked toward the bathroom. "Matty," he said again.

Maybe she was sick, he thought. He could hear her heaving. At the bathroom door, he turned the knob, only to find it locked. He listened, and when he heard her crying, he banged on the door. He felt his stomach tighten.

"Matty," he yelled. The door opened slowly. Jorge

knelt down in front of her. She was crumpled on the floor, her cheeks streaked with tears. Her long eyelashes clumped together, her eyeshadow smudged, and her nose red. "Baby, what? What happened?"

Matilde had looked into his pretty brown eyes and began to cry again.

He cupped her face in his large hands, shushed her, and then smoothed her hair. He handed her some toilet paper and watched as she wiped her eyes and nose. He held his breath when she finally looked up at him. "Matty, please tell me what's wrong? Qué pasó?"

Matilda told Jorge about Eva, that Eva lost the baby.

"The baby . . . the baby was dead," she said, squeezing Jorge's arm. The word "baby" caught him off guard. He forced himself to listen, to understand. He exhaled when he realized it was someone else's baby.

"Eva, from next door," she said.

He had nodded; he knew the girl. Matilde's mascara left long black streaks across her pale cheeks. Jorge wiped them gently away with his thumbs. She kept squeezing the toilet paper into a ball, then tearing it open.

"The ba—" she started to say, shuddered, and cried again.

He had pulled on the roll of toilet paper and handed her more. He stroked her cheek and tucked a stray hair behind her ear. He watched her for a long time. He wanted to make it better for her, to heal her heart. Hell, mend his own. He wondered if it would always be that way. Would their grief always catch them by surprise? She reached for him again. He had watched her face, dark eyes, searching his, looking for the comfort he couldn't offer. He stood, letting her hand slide gently down his arm. He walked out. This time, she would have to find her way out of the pain, alone.

When the last baby almost killed her, Jorge had said no more. IniTíally, they cried together, and for months afterward, she kept on crying. Jorge would hug her tightly, kiss her softly until she quieted down. One evening, as tears slid down her cheeks while she was cooking, he glanced at her, and just as she was expecting him to wrap his thick body around her, he left the kitchen. He walked away then as he did now. He could not imagine the depth of her grief, but he knew his.

They stopped trying after the third miscarriage. At thirty, she was still a young woman. They agreed no more. No more trying. No more lovemaking in the hope of a baby. Just no more. She was on the pill. Every morning with her first glass of water at seven-thirty, Jorge handed her a handful of vitamins, and discreetly among them was the pill. He gave her the pill because he needed to know that when he reached out to love her, he wouldn't eventually kill her.

He remembered watching her take the pill the first couple of times. He was embarrassed by how much he needed to see her take it. He forced himself to look and walk away. The pill had felt like his salvation. The thought of it made him breathe easier.

One morning, as she stood by the kitchen entrance brushing her hair, she asked, "Amor, can you get all my pills together?" He had been filling his cup with coffee.

"Por favor," she said. There was a strain, a forced cheeriness in her voice that she used with their friends when she really didn't want to do something but didn't know how to tell them.

He turned to look at her. He put the coffee cup down on the counter harder than he intended, making the coffee slosh onto his hand and counter. He ran his hand quickly under the cool water from the faucet.

She had iniTíally made a big production of keeping the pills on the kitchen counter and not in the bathroom like Jorge imagined most women did. *She needed the reminder. She didn't want to forget.* He had gotten used to them there on the counter by the big bottles of vitamin C and E. He avoided touching them.

She had stopped brushing her hair as she waited for his answer.

"No," he said.

Pretending she didn't hear him keeping her voice in that false happy octave, "Por favor, amor," she continued. "Can you do this for me? I need you to do this for me." She was gripping her hair tightly.

He looked at her intently. He did not want to do this. The smile on her was fading, and her eyes shined. Por favor, she had said again as her hand that held the brush trembled. He knew that if he did not give her the pill, she might not take it. The image of the blood and the rush to the hospital let him know that he would do this, have to do it—for him, not her. And she wouldn't care or know the difference as long as he did it.

Breathing deeply, Jorge tried to push away the memories of those awful days. He tried to forget the anger he felt at Matilde for making him give her the pill. He washed the dishes, scrubbed and wiped the counters, wiped the stove, and threw the cheap aluminum dented pot in the garbage. If he could just concentrate, he knew he could get through the moment. He looked at the dining table set for dinner and grew desperate to get to before—*before* Matilde heard about this baby, *before* this girl was pregnant, *before* they knew they would be childless.

He met Matilde at a church flea market his mother, Consuelo, had organized. Matilde was setting out miniature cat figurines at the table next to his mother's. Her long hair cascaded down one side as she bent over and took the figurines out of the box a few at a time. Jorge had bought his mother and her friends coffee and pastries from the Mexican shop around the corner from the church. The ladies gathered around him, taking their choice of coffees and treats as his mother noticed him staring at Matilde.

"Matilde," Consuelo said, "this is my son, Jorge." Matilde stood up, flipped, and gathered her hair to one side, and smiled at Jorge. He mumbled, "Hi," recovered quickly, and offered to help her unload her box.

Consuelo stood near them and said, "Matilde just joined our church." Consuelo had a twinkle in her eye as she watched them. Jorge went to church to get Matilde to go out with him for breakfast. She said yes after the fifth time.

On their first date, they sat in the corner booth of Rudy's Diner. A pretty, shaved-head waitress took their order.

Matilde stared at her in awe. "Does it feel good?" Matilde asked the waitress, looking at her head.

"Yes," the waitress said with a big smile on her face as she walked away with their order.

"Are you thinking of cutting your hair?" asked Jorge.

"This is already short."

Jorge's eyes widened as he gazed at her almost waist-length hair.

"I grew up in a very strict religious household. I couldn't wear pants, have short hair, or date. I went to church six days a week. My father was an assistant pastor. We had to be a model family."

"I can't imagine. My mother is very church-going, but she never forced it on me."

Matilde shrugged her shoulders. "You were lucky. My life was school and church. As I got older, it was then work and church. I wanted to go to college, but my parents forbade it. I remember being very upset. I didn't want to leave the church. I just wanted to know the world better." She took a sip of her tea and looked out the diner's streaked window. She told him how her father, Alberto, had suddenly died of a stroke, and her mother, Ursula, fell apart and seemed to need more of Matilde. Matilde took on all the cleaning and cooking for them both. "All I remember of that time was how tired I was."

When Ursula hinted that Matilde could support them both on her salary, she simply said no. Her mother, used to cowering, didn't push back. "I think that's when I decided I had to leave."

The waitress brought their orders. She looked at it for so long that he thought she was saying grace. She looked up and smiled, her eyes brimming with tears. "A year after my father died, I got promoted from receptionist to office manager. I kept the extra income in a separate account and didn't tell my mother.

"I started hanging out with my co-workers, telling mother I was working late. I was amazed at how easy the lies came to me. I bought myself modern clothes, telling mother that I had to look professional to be considered for a promotion and bring home more money."

She chuckled. "I even bought myself lip gloss, which I only wore at work. She must have known or guessed; several times a week, I could hear her pray ing for my soul. My mother told me I was headed down the path of sin."

She told Jorge that when she got her hair cut with the help of her co-worker, Wanda, her mother grew hysterical. Her hair was past her butt, and she had gotten it cut to just above her elbows. Before Matilde could calm her down, her mother had called the church elders.

Pastor Ernesto Mercado and his wife, Rosa, sat across from her on the dining room table. Daniella, the church secretary, sat next to her mother on the sofa, soothing her hands. The pastor and his wife were both short and round. The pastor had laid the Bible on the table. Rosa sat with her hands across her expansive stomach and looked at Matilde over the rim of her bifocal glasses. "I don't remember what they said. I'm sure they quoted several Bible verses, and we must have all prayed together. I listened respectfully, but I knew that night that I was never going back to church. And I knew I had to leave my mother's home immediately."

"Where did you go?"

"The next day, I put one change of clothes in my large purse; that's all that could fit. I stayed with my friend Wanda and her family for a few days until I found a room with Doña Mimi. She needed help paying the rent. The room was neat and clean; it was everything I needed."

He reached for her hand.

"I want you to know the kind of woman that I am," she said. "Y tú?"

He looked away, embarrassed. He was thirty-one and had managed to do very little with his life. "I don't have a story for you yet." He knew immediately that if he wanted to be with Matilde, he would have to do and want more. And, over time, Matilde had shown him who he really was: a man full of dreams and utterly capable of pursuing them. She became his driving force.

ِِِذِ

He pounded the counter with his fist. He closed his eyes and waited for the anger to subside. Instead, he remembered the ugly green walls of the hospital as he paced, waiting to hear about Matty.

The first, she felt pain, severe cramps, then suddenly blood and the rush to the hospital. The second, he had gotten a call at work. He was relieved when he saw her face. Jorge was surprised. He didn't even know she was pregnant. "I only suspected this morning," she had said to him. He sunk his head down on the hospital bed, by her hip, and wept as she stroked his thick hair.

The third time, she whispered his name and grabbed his arm. He woke from a nightmare where he was drowning, gasping for air and his heart pounding. The sheets were soaked with blood. He called 911, wrapped her in a blanket, carried her down to the lobby, and waited for the ambulance. She was pale and unconscious when he laid her on the gurney. He closed his eyes and listened to the whirring of the siren above the ambulance as it sped to the hospital, praying that she would be okay.

That third and final time he came home from the hospital, all he thought about was how he couldn't lose her. As the wind howled around him, he had grown determined; he would take care of her and help her heal. He turned onto Simpson and could see his building in the distance and quickened his steps. When he stepped in, the warmth of the building overwhelmed him. He rubbed his hands together and was grateful to finally be home. As he rode the elevator up to the fourth floor, he was making a plan—talk to the doctors, make sure she was eating well and resting. They would get through this together. When he walked into their bedroom and smelled the metallic scent of blood and saw the burgundy stain in the middle of their mattress, he decided no more.

They were finally settling into a new life routine. Most nights, he made dinner. Friday nights, they went dancing at one of their favorite salsa clubs and woke up late on Saturday mornings. They ate breakfast, made love, watched a movie, and eventually got out of bed. He would get in a game of basketball and then lift weights at the gym, and she shopped, maybe did laundry, and made plans with friends for Saturday night. If he put in enough overtime, they planned a summer week at the beach. And, if things were really good, a week in Puerto Plata visiting his extended family. And now this.

He heard her crying again and grew angry. He would not, could not comfort her. He knew what she wanted. He wanted a family with Matilde but not at the risk of losing her. He didn't know how to reconcile her need for a baby, at any cost, and his need for her.

He had tried to bring up adoption, only to be disappointed by her refusal and antiquated way of thinking. He had mentioned this to Matilde not long after the third time as she made grilled cheese sandwiches.

"I've been thinking. I know having a family is important to us. What about adoption? We can talk to Mercalis, from the first floor. She just adopted her son."

He saw the look of disgust that came over her face. "God will not deny me," she said, her voice loud and forceful as she banged the spatula on the counter. "He . . . he owes me?"

He had never seen her so angry or irrational. "God? You think this is God?" he asked, his voice rising. "Which God is this? The one that saved you from your crazy mother or the one that made her your mother in the first place?"

She moved back from the stove, her voice pleading, whiny, "But I want to be a real mother."

"Listen to yourself. You think Melcalis, who adopted her son, is not a real mother? What about Doña Mimi, whom we visit and take care of her like she is *your* mother because she saved you, loved you, who you even call Mamá? I hope she never hears you say something so selfish."

She ran out of the kitchen.

This broke his heart.

That's when he stopped consoling her. Had he been wrong about Matilde? He had thought of her as open, loving, and kind. He was not prepared for her archaic way of thinking. It was a way to get what they wanted—to have a child, to grow their family. It was a path out of the pain. Why couldn't she see it?

When he confided in his mother, Consuelo, she said, "I know you think she saved you, but you saved her." She handed him a cafecito in a mug.

He looked at his mother in astonishment. He had been in such need of direction and focus when he met Matilde that this had not occurred to him. He took a sip and burned his tongue.

"She needed you as much as you needed her."

He tried to see the truth in what his mother was saying. She was leaning by the sink, rinsing out the greca.

As he was leaving his mother's apartment that day, she said, "Ella no es el premio."

"Qué?"

"Stop worshipping her like she's a prize you won. See her, all of her. That way you can better love her."

ↄℓↄ

He gathered the groceries that she dropped when she ran in. He hadn't realized that the glass orange juice bottle had cracked. There was a small puddle of juice. He picked up the pieces of broken glass carefully. Matilde bent down to help him. She had changed into one of his old t-shirts and her pajama bottoms. Her hair was gathered in a loose bun. They worked quietly. She put away the groceries. He cleaned up the floor. He was afraid to look at her. He

was afraid to see what he knew he would, her desire to try
again. He was not ready.

Matilde walked up behind him and wrapped her arms
around him, leaned her face on his back. He held onto her
hands for a long time. He loved her. He needed her. He
couldn't get around this, and he didn't want to. He was trying to bring himself to where she was—to that clean white
place where hope still existed.

"Jorge."

He shook his head no. "Not now, Matty." He needed
more time. More time to digest that he would acquiesce.
That he would do as she asked, even if it might kill her. He
let go of her hands and walked onto the terrace. His love
felt warped and desperate, and he knew no other way.

That night, they laid back-to-back in bed. Matilde finally turned around and put her arm on his. "Jorge," she
whispered, "this life that we are making for ourselves, I
thought I was okay with. I love you more than anything.
I can see you trying hard to make me happy. And still I want
more, and I really didn't know how much until this afternoon.

He turned to face her.

"All I was thinking was bringing home your orange
juice and sneaking in a tin of Sara Lee pound cake."

He smiled. He knew how much she loved it.

"When Altagracia said the baby was born dead and how
much Eva had screamed, I could barely breathe. I ran out of
the bodega and almost knocked down old Gregorio. I just
wanted to be home with you. When I stepped into the bathroom and noticed how clean it was, I cried. *Is that it*, I wondered. A clean home and our little routines. It's important to
me that it be our baby—mine and yours, made from us."

He sighed. "Matty, the last time … you almost—" He
wouldn't say it, stopped himself from thinking it. "I held
you, carried you downstairs. I knew I wanted you alive
more than I wanted a baby."

She put her arms around him. He nuzzled close to her
breast, and the tears fell easily down his face. Her arms
tightened around him.

The next morning, Jorge woke up stiff and groggy as Matty stirred beside him. He got up and headed for the bathroom and hoped the shower would wake him up and give him the energy he needed to make a life-altering decision. After he dressed, he stood by the kitchen counter, looking at the bottles of vitamins and the little packet of pills. He reached for it, held it in his hands; he could throw it in the garbage; instead, he opened the drawer beside his hip and placed it inside. He could feel a slight tingle in his hands.

و

It had taken them a while to go back to spontaneous love-making; the best times were when he sat out on the terrace and she'd come out, lean down, and place her chin on the crook of his neck, her long hair covering his chest and the newspaper he was reading.

"Jorge," she would whisper, "come inside."

"Matty, let a man read."

"Oh Jorge, come on," she said as she slid her hand slowly down his chest.

He stopped her hand just before it reached his crotch. She laughed loudly, drawing attention from the neighbors out on their terraces. He gave her a small peck on her lips, and with his other arm, pulled her onto his lap and she laughed again, quieter as her eyes glistened with excitement. Slowly she kissed his neck, all the while drawing small circles on his forearm with her finger. Standing suddenly, her eyes filled with desire, her voice soft yet authoritative, she would say, "Jorge, come inside." He didn't even try to resist. He followed her inside; sometimes all they did was pull the curtain and make love on the living room floor. Other times, he chased her into the bedroom with her squealing and him grunting like a caveman.

They were creating another life now, one that did not include children or the mourning of not having them. At least that's what he thought before all of this. He had not realized how much his morning routine, his new life, depended on hearing the little pill pop out of its holder. For three years now, that small pill had set their life right. It hadn't been something he had wanted to do, but once he started, he felt relieved. How could he suddenly give that up?

He gulped down his vitamins with a glass of water, refilled the glass, and took the packet from the drawer where he had just hidden it. The pressure of this thumb against the packet was inviting. He heard the shower stop; she would be out soon. He wanted to be the man she wanted and needed him to be, but he was frightened. What if she miscarried again? What if it killed her? What if he had to live without her? The last thought terrified him most of all. Matilde had brought so much order and laughter into his life; he couldn't go back to loneliness again. He didn't know how to reconcile her need for a baby and his fear of living without her.

Jorge handed her the glass of water and the handful of vitamins. Jorge put his arms around Matilde's shoulder and held her close. He looked at the smooth slope of her nose and caressed her cheek. He loved her more than he ever thought himself capable of loving. She looked up at him and smiled.

Eva

Eva stands in front of the full-length mirror, trying to avoid looking at her belly. In the mirror's reflection, she sees the mess that is her bedroom. She should clean it, but all she can do right now is look at herself. She smooths down her frizzy hair, but it springs back up. She is disoriented. She is having a hard time recognizing herself. Her t-shirt is caught under her bra strap, exposing some of her belly. This brings her back. The stretch marks and scratches are clear. She knows who she is and what has happened.

Here at home, she doesn't have the benefit of disappearing into the brick wall that faced her hospital window. Every brick, crevice, and crack, a whole universe to disappear into. Here, she is among her things, and at every turn, she comes back, is present, and remembers. She isn't trying to disappear or even forget. She finds the space between here and there alluring. In that in-between space, there is no pain or color, just a gray amorphous cloud in which she floats.

She was surprised when she found out she was pregnant, but she was happy; she was always happy. She loved her baby from the moment she knew. She had no idea what kind of father Marco would be, and she knew that she would be a good mother. She learned that from her grand-

mother, Celeste. Doris, her mother, had decided that moth-
erhood was not for her. She left Eva at four in Celeste's care
and barely looked back.

Doris appeared for the oddest events—a neighbor's
funeral, Eva's eleventh birthday, and Celeste and Papito's
wedding anniversary, even though Papito had been dead
for fifteen years. These visits confused both Celeste and
Eva. Why does she come, Eva had once asked Celeste. "I
think to check to see if she made the right choice."

They knew not to expect Doris on milestone birthdays,
graduations, or even Celeste's fortieth year of sobriety celebration. On that day, Eva surprised Celeste. She took
her grandmother to the diner for breakfast, gave a heart-
shaped gold locket that had taken her six months to pay off
on layaway and flowers. "Ay, m'ija," was all Celeste managed to say as she cried.

The scratches remind Eva that she had failed at mother-
hood much more spectacularly than her own mother. She
had not abandoned her baby. She had given birth to a dead
baby. Eva touches her belly. It is soft, fluffy, and sore.
The scratches are still red and tender. She pulls the t-shirt
down. When the nurse asked if she wanted to hold him, she
thought no, but couldn't say it. The tears slid down the side
of her eyes and into her ears. She could not imagine seeing
and feeling him for only one time. So she denied herself.
The nurse patted her hands and left Eva to her bricks outside the hospital window.

She feels the gray mist gathering around her, and she
closes her eyes for a moment. When she opens them, she
sees Marco's thick, shiny gold-link chain on her bookshelf.
She turns to look at it to make sure it isn't a trick her mind
is playing on her. It is there. It sits in a tight coil. She picks
it up. It is cool and heavy. The last time he was there, they
laid on the bed. He was on his stomach, and she on her side.

"Scratch my back," he said, turning to face her with a
small smile on his face.

She very gently raked her nails from his shoulders

down to his hip in long strokes. Her hand moved across his skin slowly back and forth from right to left, then left to right, each time avoiding his spinal column because it felt odd to touch the small curve of it. Marco turned to face her with a satisfied smile. He reached up, kissed her softly, then rested back on the bed. She used his arm as a pillow and they both fell asleep. When she awoke, he was gone, having forgotten his chain. She began to cry.

The day she met Marco, she felt a sense of relief. She spent so much of her time waiting, waiting for something, almost anything, to happen. So when he took the bags from her hand with his dazzling smile, all she could do was smile back. There had been boys and friends. She had just started her first semester at college, and all of that was interesting in a way. And still she seemed to be expecting something. Everything left her just a bit unsatisfied, and she wasn't quite sure why.

"Hi," he said a little too loudly as he took the grocery bags from her. His eyes had a hint of green and yellow with specks of brown in them. They crinkled as his smile widened and a dimple appeared on his left cheek. His brown skin seemed to glow. *Finally*, she thought as he stepped in the elevator with her; something was happening. She was both relieved and excited.

Once in the elevator with him, she backed herself into a corner as he pressed the fourth-floor button without her having to say it.

"Where do you work?" he asked.

"At a lawyer's office, as a receptionist." She stepped forward. Whatever was about to happen she wanted to be up close to it.

"You going to school?"

"I just started at City College."

"Smart," he said, smiling.

"Of course," she said with a smirk.

He raised an eyebrow.

She blushed, turned away, and then smiled. She was surprised to see how beautiful his smile was. His teeth were perfectly square, his thick lips a reddish-brown and a little wet because he had just licked them. When they reached her apartment, he placed the bag by the door and said, "See you around, Eva."

The next few times she saw him, he would be standing in front of her building. "What's up?" he would say.

She smiled and said nothing and continued on her way upstairs. She would obsess about those short exchanges for days. What he wore, how he looked, who he was with. Was he waiting for her, or did he happen to be standing there as she came home? Finally, on a Friday afternoon, he said, "Eva, what are you doing tonight?" And without waiting for her to answer, he said, "Let's go to the movies. I'll come get you around seven." And that's how it started; he'd take her to movies, twice they walked around 42nd Street and watched how the tourists marveled at the lights, traffic, and New Yorkers. Once, they were near her job, and she pointed to the building where she worked.

He surprised her one day and waited for her in front of the office. He wore a brand-new Yankee cap, a navy-blue t-shirt, Levi's jeans, and Jordans. He had a thick rope gold chain that came down to his chest. He looked very serious until he saw her. His smile made her stomach flutter, and she couldn't help but smile back. He kissed her, just as the girls that she worked with — who ignored her because they were assistants, and she merely the receptionist — came out. Red-haired Patricia gasped, and tall, skinny, wannabe-model Robin just stared at her and then at Marco. He stared at both women, and they looked away hurriedly. After that, they invited her to lunch and were friendlier, but Eva always declined.

Thinking about Marco makes her smile. She walks back to her dresser, picks up the big-tooth comb, and grabs her ponytail. Her thick, long hair often overwhelmed her. Marco always told her to do it a little at a time. He would sit on the edge of the bed as she sat between his legs, crossed-legged on the floor as though they were mother and child. He would take her hair in chunks and, with the comb, go at each section gingerly, removing the tangles until the comb would move through her hair smoothly. She asked him once, "Where did you learn this?"

"Mami and Papi. She had hair like yours. Papi would untangle it for her. I loved to watch them." He stopped de-tangling her hair, lost in thought. She looked up at him, his face smooth, and his eyes had a faraway look.

"She wasn't as tender-headed as you," he said, bring-ing himself back. He handed Eva a section of untangled hair. She squeezed out a bit of Vitapointe hair cream from a small tube and rubbed it in and then braided the section. When it was all done, he laughed at her, with her thick ev-ery-which-way braids. She begged him not to laugh, which made him laugh harder. The laughter dissolved into kissing and then lovemaking.

She looks at herself in the mirror again. She isn't sure she could do it, comb her hair, shower, clean, live. Every-thing is so hard, and the quiet space beckons. And although she isn't pregnant, she feels like she is carrying a stone in her stomach.

※

At the hospital, she woke to find her hands restrained. The room was dark. Marco had pulled a chair close to her bed. He slept with half of his body on her legs. When he felt her move, he sat up. Eva, he whispered. He stood, took out his pocketknife, and cut the ties that held her hands. She tried to sit up.

"No, no," he said, keeping his voice low. He leaned down and they held each other. She shuddered and then let him go.

"I'm sorry," she finally said. "Help me sit up," her voice hoarse. She moaned a little as she moved. She held onto his arm as he hit the up button on the side of the bed, and the mattress rose slowly. She noticed the red and brown stains in the front of her gown. She went to touch it, stopped, and looked at him.

"You … you started screaming, pulling, and scratching yourself," he said, looking at the reddish-brown stain on her gown.

"I want to see."

Marco pulled the covers and helped her lift up her gown. Her abdomen was bandaged. She didn't remember screaming or scratching. She remembered the skinny doctor standing next to her grandmother. His mouth was moving. Her grandmother squeezed her hand and cried. And then she was in this quiet opaque place, floating. When she opened her eyes, she was in a dark hospital room, and Marco's arms were wrapped around her legs. What would they do now? They had all sorts of plans. Arranging their dead son's funeral had not been one of them.

Last Christmas, Eva and Celeste were having breakfast among all the decorations. She looked at the scattered ornaments, took a deep breath, squeezed the mug her grandmother had just given her filled with a sweet cafe con leche, and said, "I'm pregnant." Eva watched her grandmother's face and marveled at its stillness. Only her eyes moved, first down at her cafecito, then up and past Eva toward the half-assembled Christmas tree. She sighed. "Tell Marco to come for dinner," she finally said as she got up to go to the kitchen.

"I told her about the baby," Eva told Marco later that day as they sat in the park behind the building that faced Tiffany Street. They huddled together against the cold.

"Was she angry?"

"I think she's sad." Eva was quiet for a moment. "She wants you to come over for dinner."

"What?"

"She wants us to talk about it, like a family."

"Family?"

She noticed the hesitation in his voice. "We're a family now."

"Right, right," he responded.

When Marco came to dinner, Eva grabbed his hand. It was cold and sweaty. Eva had never seen Marco nervous. He was dressed all in black — black t-shirt, black jeans, and black sneakers. His gold chain was tucked underneath his t-shirt.

"Hi," he said shyly, his voice low and boy-like, "Doña Celeste."

"Hola amor," Celeste said. "Ven siéntate."

He sat on the edge of the long plastic-covered couch, his left leg bouncing up and down. Eva set the table for three as Celeste finished up in the kitchen. Eva watched Marco look around the room. She realized that they never sat in the living room. He had always just slipped into her bedroom when Celeste was at work or shopping. He was smiling at Eva's school pictures.

As they sat around the table, Eva realized she was also nervous as she served herself watercress salad. They had all begun to eat quietly. Eva watched as Marco put a forkful of red beans and rice in his mouth slowly and then raised his eyebrows. *At least he liked the food*, thought Eva.

"Congratulations," Celeste said and put her fork down. Eva and Marco looked up.

"This is not what I wanted for you, Eva. I had hoped that you would finish college before starting a family." She shrugged her shoulders. "Pero aquí estamos."

"I'll take care of her," said Marco.

"I expect no less from Indio's son."

Marco's eyes narrowed. "You know — knew — my father."

"Of course," she said. "We all knew him. He was so handsome and had a pretty smile. Era un hombre respetuoso. And very helpful. See that chinero, behind you? He helped fix it." She looked away. "You must have been a baby. I saw him one day in the street and told him that there was something wrong with the legs; it kept tilting, and I couldn't figure it out. Mostly, I was afraid it would come crashing down. Papito was sick by then, so he couldn't fix it. Indio

came over with his toolbox and spent two hours right there."
She pointed to the middle of the living room. "He made Papito get out of bed to ask his advice. He asked Papito what
kind of glue or nail he should use. Should he start from
the bottom, remove the shelf? He removed the doors, the
shelves, and adjusted the legs, all under Papito's supervision.
He made Papito test its sturdiness. Indio knew what to do,
but he also knew what it meant for another man to come into
your home to fix something only a few months ago you could
have done yourself. It made Papito feel good for days afterward. He helped Papito forget he was dying. I will always be
grateful for that. Your father was a good man." Celeste was
silent for a long time. "Como se va el tiempo."

Marco looked at the cabinet.

"¿Qué vamos hacer?" Celeste looked at them.

"The baby is due at the end of the summer," Eva said.
"I was thinking that I would take the fall semester off. And
maybe with your help," she hesitated, "I could go back to
school next Spring."

"I'm relieved you're still thinking about school. And, of
course, I'll help take care of the baby."

"I'll pay you to babysit," said Marco.

"No," Celeste said sternly. "That's my great grandbaby;
you will not pay me to help raise it. You will help provide
and be there."

He nodded, looked down, and then sat up straight.

"Have you told your Tía?"

"Not yet."

"I'm sure she will be very happy."

"You think?" Again, Eva noticed that his voice had a
little boy quality to it.

"She loves you. She worries about you. And now I will
worry about you."

"I'll be fine." His voice deepened.

"I hope so. I expect you to be as good a father to this
baby as Indio was to you."

Marco's brown skin deepened in color. He looked away
and swallowed the mouth full of rice and beans.

"It was clear that he adored you both."

"I loved him too," Marco said, his voice low.

><

"I saw him," Marco said in the hospital room. The hospital streetlight cast a long shadow in her room. He was in the dark half. "He's perfect. He has your hair." He started to smile and stopped.

"I wanted to hold him, but I was afraid."

He dragged the chair closer. She could see his face clearly.

"I did take his tiny hand and hold it," he said, sitting back and falling into the darkness. "I wanted him to know me. I wanted to know him. It's stupid."

"It's not stupid. I couldn't . . . I couldn't," she cried, covering her mouth with her hands.

He climbed into bed with her and held her. She leaned her head against his chest.

"I wanted to name him after my father," he said.

This startled Eva. She hadn't thought about giving him a name. "Are you sure?"

"Yes."

"But ..."

"You never talk about your father. We could add his name as a middle name."

"I don't know who my father is. I don't know anything about him, not even his name."

Marco turned to look at her. "I'm sorry."

Eva shrugged.

"What about Papito's name?"

She leaned away from him. There was something wrong in naming a dead child in honor of other dead people. Maybe if their son had lived, but this felt wrong to her, and she didn't know how to say this to Marco. "Marco, do you want to save your father's name?"

"Save it?"

"Yes, our baby is dead. You may have other children, another son, maybe ..." He stood up abruptly.

She struggled to sit up.

"What are you saying?"

In a halting voice, she said, "I want your father's name to live on. And our baby, our baby . . . didn't. Maybe one day you'll have another son, and you may want to name him after your father."

He began to pace in the room.

"Marco," she said, stretching out her hand.

"He is my baby too."

"Yes." She pleaded with him to get closer. She could see the pain flash on and off his face as he stepped in and out of the darkness. "Marco, I just want ..."

"What? This is our baby, Eva."

"I know. I only meant that you might have another chance one day." She began to cry. "Don't waste it on a dead baby."

He stopped pacing. "You fucking bitch."

"Marco, please, please try to understand what I'm saying."

"Fuck you," were his final words to her. She saw the cruel smile on his face as he left.

Eva starts to gently undo her long braid. She is determined to detangle and wash her hair. She can feel Marco's chain by her thigh. She looks down at it. Is this all she has of him? She sees the two pairs of sneakers he gave her: K-Swiss and high-top gray Nikes that she hates. She is devastated about the baby. When she thinks of what could have been a hazy cloud envelops her. In that place she is unseen from furtive, pitiful glances. It is a quiet place. There are no sirens, no crying grandmothers or whispers. There is only a soft hum. It is weightless and she is free to be.

Her grandmother walks in and sits next to her. Eva is surprised to see her there. She expects her grandmother to say something about the state of her room, the funk coming off her body, her hair.

"We'll get through this," Celeste says.

Eva leans on her grandmother's shoulders. She feels

the coolness of her grandmother's skin and begins to cry again. From where she sits, Eva cannot see herself in the mirror. The reflection reveals the chaotic state of her room. Clothes, schoolbooks, and papers everywhere. She sees the crib still in its box, tilting oddly against the wall. Marco's plan was to put it together this weekend. Next to the crib are the four boxes of diapers her grandmother gave her. The baby clothes she couldn't resist buying are still in their store bags. A six-pack of baby bottles, baby oil, and shampoo are all in a small yellow baby tub haphazardly arranged on top of the diapers. It looks as though it could all topple at any moment. Her whole life turned upside down in the span of a week. First, she is a mother-to-be, a future ahead of her, now her baby and Marco are dead.

Eva stops crying, stands abruptly, and screams. This is not what she wanted. Where is her baby? Where is Marco? The scream pours out of her like a howl. Her grandmother calls her name, but she can't hear her. Confused, she runs toward the mirror to grab the baby things. She turns. Celeste tries to grab her arms. Eva pushes her away. She rushes to the corner with all of the baby items. She grabs the bags of clothes, holds them close to her chest, and runs past her grandmother toward the terrace.

Celeste goes after and then freezes when she sees Eva on her tippy toes on the edge of the terrace. "Eva!"

Eva hears her grandmother cry out, "Nooo, m'ija," but she flings the bag of clothes anyway. She goes back, pushing her grandmother aside, and grabs the tub and bottles, runs back to the terrace, and throws it all over the railing. She goes back for the boxes of diapers. Her grandmother tries to stop her again, ripping a box open. Eva hurls the box over the terrace. For a moment, she watches the diapers fall like large pieces of cotton candy. She sees that people have gathered below. She turns back for more.

"Eva," someone yells so loud, she actually halts in the living room. Someone is in front of her, but she can't make out who it was. Then she feels the sharp sting of a slap. She blinks and sees Doña Elli.

"I know, sweetheart."

No. Eva shakes her head. No one knows. No one un-
derstands. Her baby, her baby is dead. She is trying to get
around Doña Elli.

"My baby died too. She was so tiny, so precious. I
loved her more than I loved God."

Eva listens.

"She was, for a long time, the only thing I was most
proud of in my life." Doña Elli lets go of Eva. They look
into each other's eyes and weep.

The next few days, Eva spends in a fog, but in the back-
ground, she can hear Doña Elli talking to her grandmother.
She hears her grandmother crying when she shows Doña
Elli the bag of pills the doctors have prescribed for her. Eva
is trying hard to remember when she had even gone to the
doctor. The soft space kept calling, and she kept going.

Eva feels herself being taken to the living room and
being made to stand. Around her are small points of light.
Someone places a chain around Eva's neck and dabs a scent
behind her ears, wrist, and chest. It smells of citrus and
cinnamon. She is surrounded by smoke; there are prayers
and words she does not understand being said in loud voices. The voices grow loud, so loud she puts her hands over
her ears. Someone's hand gently moves them. She is turned
around and around. Each time, the smoke and fragrance
grow intense. She can feel a spray of water on her face.

The mist disappears, and in front of her stands her
grandmother, Doña Elli, and Doña Anita. At first, she feels
a discomfort in her abdomen. The feeling grows until the
pain is sharp and clear. It expands to her chest. It intensi-
fies; she doubles over and cries out. All three women step
forward to grab her. This happens every Friday for a month
at sunset.

On that last Friday, Eva sits on the couch, tired from
what has happened, and watches as the ladies clean up.
Doña Anita moves the candles up from the floor, making

sure to keep them lit, and puts them on the table. Doña Elli opens up the terrace door to clear the air of the cigar smoke. Her grandmother removes the rosary from around Eva's neck. Then they all sit eating thick slices of pound cake that Doña Anita made with tea and coffee. They fill the living room with laughter and neighborhood gossip. Eva manages to smile.

"I buried him in his baptismal clothes," said Celeste.

Eva nodded.

"Elli, Anita and I did a novena for him."

Eva has spent days in a stupor from the medication. She could see what was happening around her but couldn't react to it. There are moments she wants to scream and cry, but the feelings seem to be trapped in her chest. First, she is touching his baptismal clothes; next, she is at the gravesite. There were whispers about Marco and the police, and then, nothing. Between the Friday night rituals with the ladies and her grandmother reducing the dosages of her medications, she starts to remember. She remembers her baby; she remembers Marco. The grief feels like falling into an abyss. When she thought she couldn't get out, there were the ladies—Doña Elli, Doña Anita, and her grandmother. Their arms outstretched, pulling her forward. They held her hand, hugged her, let her cry on their shoulders, and sleep on their laps. They combed her hair, made her eat, and watched her sleep.

"I don't know what to do now."

"Live." Celeste held her hand. "Marco ..."

"Is dead."

Her grandmother gave her a quizzical look.

"He came to me in a dream. I saw blood on his chest," she says, rubbing her own. "He reached his hands out to me, and I tried to grab it, but the distance between us kept growing and growing. And then he was so far away that I couldn't see him anymore."

The thought of Marco's beautiful face still gave her

butterflies. She cries for him late at night. She hadn't realized how much she loved him. She remembers his confident
walk, the stern face that faded quickly the minute he saw
her. She misses the pressure of his body on hers, the tight
hugs, the way he just threw his arm around her, both claim-
ing and bringing her close to him. She grins at the memory
of the first time they had sex. He must have thought that
she was a virgin; he was gentle. The look of surprise as she
wrapped her legs around his waist and arched her back.
They never talked about it, but she caught him a few times
looking at her with wonder and curiosity. He was good to
her, but she knew that wasn't always the case with others,
even with Lorenzo.

Lorenzo came to see her twice. The first time, she pretend-
ed to be asleep. She didn't want to see him. She didn't want
to talk about the baby or Marco with him. The second time,
the ladies were visiting. He tried to walk out, but Celeste
pulled him in.

"Muchacho," says Anita, "tu estas muy flaco. Quédate
para el almuerzo."

"No se apure."

"Claro que sí," says Celeste as Anita begins rummaging
through the refrigerator. Doña Elli points him to Eva, who
sits on the terrace enjoying the sun.

He stands by the door, unsure what to say or do. "We
buried Marco near the baby." He looks at her feet.

Eva glances up at him. He looks thin and he is skinny
to begin with. He holds a baseball cap in his hand, and his
hair is so long, it covers half his face. He shifts from foot to
foot.

"I'm sorry."

"For what?" She tries not to roll her eyes.

"Everything."

"What is everything, Lorenzo?"

His face reddens. "It's my fault. He did it on a dare."
He closes his eyes.

"Did what?"

"Talk to you?"

She stands, holds onto the railing, and says, "Do you think I'm some kind of nenita that doesn't know anything?"

He avoids her face.

"He told me."

He glances at her face and then turns to look at Doña Elli's and Domingo's empty terrace across the plaza.

"Marco told me how much you liked me. I laughed when he said that."

He winces.

"There was no way Lorenzo liked me, I told him."

Lorenzo looks at her feet again.

"If Lorenzo likes me so much, I asked him, why are *you* here? It took Marco a long time to answer me, but he did. He never lied to me. He didn't love me from far away or sneaked kisses when no one was looking." She steps closer to him.

He steps back, his face scarlet.

"I'm sorry."

"He loved you," she says, looking at him in disgust. "What did you think, that I was going to leave him for you?"

"I ... no, no ..." He trips as he steps back into the living room.

"Did you think the baby was yours?" She is in his face.

He is trying not to stumble; the wall breaks his fall.

"He was our baby," she yells. "Ours. Not yours." She wipes the tears away.

"Noo, noooo." His face seems to be collapsing into itself. He is trying not to cry.

The ladies stop to look at them. Doña Elli holds a plate in midair. Doña Anita and Celeste stare at them through the kitchen pass-through.

"Abrale la puerta, abuela."

Celeste opens the door and Lorenzo runs out.

Eva closes her eyes and takes a deep breath. When she opens them, the ladies are surrounding her.

Marco

Marco paces in the lobby. His quick steps cover its width in six short steps. He glances out the glass door. *Where is Lolo?* He is surprised it's dark out. Wasn't he just at the hospital? He shakes his head. He doesn't see drunk Esperanza stare at him then run out of the building. He barely notices old Porfila come out of her apartment with a garbage bag and then quickly turn around as though she forgot something. He thinks about Lorenzo, Eva, and his baby. He feels lost, unsure about what to do, where to go. If he could just talk to Lolo about the baby, about Eva.

The baby, the fucking baby, was gonna do it. He could finally be like his father, a man to be proud of, a man people respected. Now, he doesn't know who to become. He is leaning against the floor-to-ceiling window that looks out into the playground behind the building when the two cops walk into the building. The Latino one looks familiar. The skinny white one looks like a little boy.

"What's going on?" says the Latino cop.

Marco tries to tell them that he's okay, he's just going upstairs to see his aunt, to go home, but the words come out like a sob.

"What happened?" the Latino cop asks.

Marco puts the gun to his temple.

"Hey, hey."

The Latino cop puts his hands out in front of him.

"Lolo," Marco says in a low voice. He presses the gun hard against his temple and then drops his hand. Where could he be? Marco needs him.

The cop audibly sighs.

Marco recognizes the Latino cop. "I know you."

"Then you know I'm here to help. I'm Sergeant Ortiz."

Marco walks to the elevator and then stops. He looks down at the gun in his hand. He squints at it. He is trying to remember when he got it and sees his father's face. He means to push the call button on the elevator but doesn't. He looks at the gun again, unsure where to put it. It's heavy and slippery in his sweaty hand.

Sgt. Ortiz steps back, forcing the young cop to step back as well. "Tell me what happened, son."

"The baby . . ." He remembers how Eva shuddered and cried in his arms at the hospital.

Sgt. Ortiz nods. He stands a few feet away from the doorway with the rookie cop behind him. Sweat is staining his shirt at his chest and armpits.

"I was gonna quit. I was gonna be like Papi."

Again, Sgt. Ortiz nods and waits.

"What do I do now?"

Sgt. Ortiz gets a bit closer. "Let's figure it out."

"Eva and Lolo," Marco says just above a whisper.

"What?"

Marco is tired. He leans against the glass wall, looks down at the floor for a second, and holds the sob down that threatens to overtake him. "I wanted us to be a family. I fucked it all up."

Sgt. Ortiz takes another step.

"Lolo hates me." He starts pacing again; his gun hand swings wildly. He walks toward the garbage shoot. He hears a bag tumbling down. It lands with a thud. He walks back toward the elevator. He should have gone straight upstairs to Tía.

"Help me understand." Sgt. Ortiz takes off his cap, wipes his brow, takes another step, and puts his cap back on.

"I knew he loved her, and I wanted to hurt him. I never understood why he never talked to her. The look on Lolo's face when Iggy called out her name." He shakes his head, remembering. "I wanted us to be partners. Lolo wanted …"

Fresh tears fill Marco's eyes. All Lolo wanted was to be brothers again. "I fucked it up." After a long pause, he says, "Eva and I…" He's moving quickly from the elevator to the trash shoot. "Fuck!" He smiles and lets the tears roll down his cheeks. He's starting to understand that loving one breaks the other.

"Let's go sit down. We can try to sort it out."

Marco wants nothing more than to sit down. He wants to be with Tía in her small bedroom, telling her about his son. He wants to sink down in her overstuffed chair piled high with pillows and old bedsheets. He imagines her hand caressing his face. He moves toward Sgt. Ortiz.

Sgt. Ortiz gives Marco room to come beside him.

The tears well up again. Marco struggles to contain them. He thinks about his father and his son, and the anguish makes him moan.

Sgt. Ortiz extends his hand, reaching for Marco. The rookie cop's eyes widen.

"Fuck this shit," Marco says and points the gun to his temple again. He wipes away the tears and sweat from his face. He wants all the thoughts to go away. But first, he has to go upstairs and talk to Tía. He needs to find Lorenzo.

"No, no, we're gonna sit down and talk about it." The rookie moves from behind Sgt. Ortiz and unholsters his gun.

"Fuck this shit," Marco yells again.

There is a sudden noise at the entrance. Sr. Domingo and Pedro are falling over each other.

"The baby … the baby is dead," he wails.

The Latino cop is trying hard to focus on Marco. "What baby?"

"My baby." Marco turns back to face the cop. "My baby, my baby, died."

"What happened?" he asked as he inches closer to Marco.

"I don't know. I don't know," Marco cries. He wipes his cheeks with his gun hand. "Man, I don't know. She killed him."

"What, who?"

"It's her fault."

"How?"

"I don't know. The baby, the fucking baby was born dead," Marco screams.

Sgt. Ortiz stands still and stares at Marco. He blinks and blinks before he says, "I'm sorry."

Marco stops, sits on his haunches, and then stands quickly.

"Lolo ... I need to speak to Lolo."

"Who's Lolo?"

"My brother. I need to talk to him, tell him . . . I need to tell him the baby's name, I need to tell him . . ." The words and thoughts form only to disappear. He's looking past Sgt. Ortiz. He can see people gathered in front of the building, but none of them are Lolo.

"I'm sorry," the cop says again. "Sometimes things like this happen."

Marco looks at Sgt. Ortiz, his face softening, wanting to believe him.

"Marco," he says softly, "Give me the gun."

"I miss him."

Sgt. Ortiz nods.

"Yes, sometimes nature determines that a fetus is not viable," says the rookie cop.

Both Sgt. Ortiz and Marco look at the young white cop.

"What did you mean, my baby isn't valuable? Who the hell are you to say my son, my son," he says, pointing the gun to his chest, "that my son isn't valuable?"

"No, no, not valuable, viable—"

Sgt. Ortiz cuts the young cop off with a look.

"He had value," Marco says, his voice dropping.

Sgt. Ortiz quickly turns back to Marco. "Of course, he has value," his voice soft.

Marco's gun hand sways. "How can he say that shit? What the hell is wrong with him?" Everything starts to splinter and divide. There are four, six, eight cops instead of the two. Pedro is by the mailboxes and the door. He can see Sr. Domingo's legs and they look wrong; there are three, then six. He can see his baby's face. He blinks and sees Sgt. Ortiz is reaching for him. He lifts the gun hand and thinks, I need to tell Lolo I love him.

He stormed out of Eva's hospital room with her voice crying out to him. How could Eva not want to name the baby after his father? He stood in front of the emergency entrance. He looked around. He began to walk toward the street but found that he didn't know where to go. He began to walk back and forth in front of the automatic doors. They would open, almost close, and start to open again. He was cursing and yelling at Eva. He hated her. He loved her. How could she do this to him? His breathing labored, his brow furrowed, and his eyes narrowed. He had to stop and bend down to catch his breath. He scanned the area for Lorenzo, but he knew Lorenzo was long gone. He let out a growl, and the security guard standing near the entrance came out to see what was the commotion. Marco saw the guard put his walkie-talkie to his mouth. He didn't care. Fuck that bitch!

Why didn't Eva understand that the baby was perfect like his father? She only knew that he was dead. She didn't know. She hadn't seen his curly jet-black hair, his flawless hand, or little mouth. She couldn't even touch him. He got out of the way of an arriving ambulance. He'd started walking to the subway by the time the guard came back with two others.

"Eva," Marco whispered over and over like a prayer on the subway ride home. There were two kinds of girls as far as he knew. Bad girls that liked bad boys. Good girls who thought they wanted the thrill of being with a bad boy until they realized what that meant—maliciousness and violence. Eva was neither. He laughed out loud. "Oh, Eva."

She treated him like a puzzle to be put together — understood and then possibly discarded. This both intrigued and scared him. He had never thought of himself as disposable. She was unafraid of him. His intensity bored her.

"If you're going to be all nasty and mean, go and save that for your boys. I don't have time for that." The first time she did that, it confused him. He left because he didn't know what to do. When she saw him next, she asked, was he better? "Good, I missed you," she said.

"Why do you do this?" she asked once as she watched him count out a stack of money. He looked up at her and then turned back to counting.

"Why do you think?"

"I don't know; that's why I'm asking." He looked at her again, her face expectant.

"The money," he said, looking down at the three stacks he had counted out so far. "Did you need the money, I mean, before?"

He thought about it for a moment. "I don't know."

"Yeah, you do." She looked at him, smiling, and then shrugged her shoulders. She always knew when he was holding back. She never pushed him, but eventually, he told her the truth. He didn't need the money, but he liked it, and the more he got, the more he wanted. The money came with power.

He told her about his parents. He had few memories of when it was just the four of them. Lolo was a fussy baby, always being held by his mother. Maria had light brown skin and hazel eyes. He smiled when he remembered her face. His dad always made breakfast on the weekends — pancakes, or farina, or oatmeal, or French toast, and always with a side of bacon. Mami loved bacon.

"What happened to her?"

"She went to rehab and never came back." She hadn't asked any more questions about his mother.

He liked laying on Eva's frilly bedspread while she rubbed his shoulders. She'd scratch his back, and he'd tell her some random story about how he and Lolo wrestled or watched kung fu movies on Saturdays.

"Why do you act like you hate him?

"I do; he's a fuckin' pussy."

"Uh-huh," she responded, looking at him with her head tilted to the side. He was lying, and they both knew it. "It sounds to me like you miss him."

"Eva," he said as he got off the subway on Simpson Street. He searched the block for Lolo. He didn't see anyone. This is what Eva called the glad-to-be-home moment. Everyone is just getting home from work, settling down, having a tranquil minute before starting their evening chores.

"Listen." They were standing on the terrace.

"What?" he asked.

"Shhh."

"I can't hear anything." The block was unusually quiet.

"Right."

He looked confused.

"You know that instant, when you get home, after a long day? Aren't you just silent; don't you just sit for a moment?"

He nodded.

"This is that moment."

He smiled and then kissed her.

He couldn't help both being angry with her about the baby's name and smiling at the thought of her. He wondered if this was love.

He headed for the apartment he shared with Iggy across from Casita Maria. He opened his dresser drawers randomly. He didn't really know what he was looking for when he saw the gun. Marco tucked it in the small of his back between his jeans and t-shirt. It felt strange, but he grew comfort from its peculiar feeling. He saw his father's MTA identification card. He touched it with his index finger and sighed. He thought of Tía. Someone had to tell her.

He rushed over. He stepped into the building and rang the doorbell over and over.

"Quien?"

"Soy yo, Tía."

"Ay, Dios Marco," he heard her say and buzzed him in.

Marco was so happy to see Lolo waiting for him in the hospital. It was early afternoon on a perfect spring day. It felt good seeing Lolo waiting there for him. He was a father. Holy shit. He couldn't even believe it. He was hoping for a son. He pulled Lolo close and hugged him. Father. Uncle. Maybe now they could be a family again. He didn't notice Lolo's long face. When he finally heard the words, it felt like cracks on thin ice had developed across his chest and spread throughout his body. He lost his breath. He could barely stand.

The doctor, the nurse, and Lolo all hovered around him. But all he could hear were Lorenzo's words echoing in his head, born dead. Each reiteration splintering the ice further.

Marco followed the doctor slowly, holding on to the wall. The fact that Lolo had been the one to tell him struck Marco as brave. They were barely speaking to each other. And there was Lolo, wanting to be there for him. Marco wanted to thank him, but he could barely look at him.

Born dead.

Worse than those words repeating endlessly was the silence when he entered the room to see his son. The light in the room was dim. It took his eyes a moment to adjust. In one corner of the room, there were discarded monitors, waiting like sentries for their marching orders. The rest of the room was empty except for the hospital bassinet.

And there he was.

His son was wrapped in a baby blanket; a few curls escaped his tiny hat. He could see the outline of his legs curled up and the arms along the sides of his body. It looked as though he were sleeping. Marco wanted to reach down and pick him up but was scared. He unwrapped the blanket and saw the baby's hand curled into a small fist. He felt the cool skin against his. He memorized the shape of his fingernails and his long, elegant eyelashes. The baby's mouth was shaped into a perfect little o. Marco's whole body shook as he cried.

He had so many questions. Where do babies go that have only known death? Is there a heaven for them? Or do they forever spiral in space with no place to go and be safe? He wished his father were there to help him. He shivered. He was hoping that he could be the father that his father had been to him, loving and patient. He remembered those mornings when he'd wake up groggy and found his dad in the living room, Lolo asleep on his lap while he read the newspaper. Papi would smile at him, drop the paper, and open his arms wide. His dad would pull him onto his lap and hug him tightly. Whatever awkwardness Marco may have felt about being a big boy and getting on his dad's lap disappeared as soon as his dad wrapped his arms around him.

Marco loved the smell of his dad; there was something metallic about it. He could smell the cold coffee on the table, and the faint smell of cigarettes lingered in the air. They walked back to the kitchen, leaving Lolo sleeping on the couch. Marco would have his donut as Papi heated up his hot chocolate in the microwave. They'd talked about the latest Hulk comic and how his math class was so boring. Papi had found a high school algebra math book and had given it to him. Marco had worked halfway through it.

Part of him wanted to stay in the hospital room forever. Pick up his perfect baby boy and curl up together. The other part wanted to run. He wanted to forget all of this. Walk away from his son, Eva, Tía, and Lolo. Start fresh somewhere else.

But how could he leave his perfect baby boy? Papi was not here to show him the way. This he would have to learn to navigate by himself. He caught the faint smell of cigarette smoke as he left the hospital room.

He searched for Lolo. Marco wanted to tell Lolo that he named the baby Gabriel, after Papi.

The Block

In retrospect, seeing old Esperanza running as fast as her chunky legs could carry her out of the building, screaming, "Ay, Dios," should have been enough to at least stop me, if for nothing else but to laugh. Old Esperanza was not really that old; she was a drunk. She shuffled around the neighborhood, reeking of alcohol and muttering to herself. And, usually at nine o'clock on any given spring and summer night, she cursed loudly at anyone who happened to be near her. Lorenzo, Iggy, Chico, and I often watched to see who would get caught in her tirade. Most neighborhood folks simply ignored her and kept walking. On rare occasions, she'd yell at a stranger that would yell right back; she'd be stunned silent. We laughed as she stared at the stranger until she couldn't see them anymore.

Seeing drunk Esperanza run out of the building should have been the first clue, but I was seriously worried about Lorenzo. Where was he? He should have been back from the hospital. The thing I knew for sure was that the baby was dead, and Lorenzo had to tell Marco.

It's funny, the things I remember about that day. Esperanza wore white athletic socks, the old school ones with the three horizontal black stripes around the top, and red

terry cloth slippers. She wore a black dress with big red
flowers on it. That's why I noticed her legs; the dress was
a little too short for her. She was of average height, like my
mother, like every woman whom I didn't really pay attention to back then. I was eighteen, full of myself, dealing
weed and sometimes crack, and catcalling girls—all while
trying hard to be cool.

Esperanza ran out screaming for God, and I just looked
at her in wonder, shook my head, and kept right on walking
to the building. Sr. Domingo and I reached for the door
handle at the same time. I was startled when I felt his hand.
Sr. Domingo was hard to miss; that should have been clue
number two. Sr. Domingo was tall, slender, very dark, and
handsome. He was the kind of man that made me wonder
if I could be like him. He was elegant with an easy smile.
The young girls grew quiet when he walked by and gave
him long, lingering glances. He had a graceful way of walking, his lean body straight, his legs extending delicately. Sr.
Domingo smiled at me as I pulled my hand away quickly.

"Pedro," Sr. Domingo asked, "y qué?" as we walked
into the building. Sr. Domingo carried three bags full of
groceries and stepped into the building first, and then
suddenly dropped the bags. I heard something break and
looked down. Sr. Domingo was on the floor. I found myself desperately trying to somehow not trip over and fall
on him. When you're big, like I was, you are always conscious of your body. You are aware of how much space you
take up in a room, in a chair, on the subway, the bus. You
are conscious of how people size you up and then move
away slowly as though you can't tell that they find your size
intimidating. That was the final clue when I looked at Sr.
Domingo in both irritation and concern. He looked horri-
fied. I finally saw what he did—two cops, one with his gun
drawn, the other with his arms outstretched—and Marco
marching across the hallway, alternating between pointing
a gun at his head and waving it around.

For a long time after, I thought about nothing else—
just that moment, not even anything beyond it. I kept reliv-

ing it in my mind as though I could have stopped it, stopped myself or Sr. Domingo from going inside. But if seeing Esperanza running out didn't stop me, nothing would. That realization alone took me months.

Sr. Domingo crawled on the floor, trying to put the escaped tomato sauce cans back into his bags. He grabbed two and pulled them close to him. He tried to back up, his right arm reaching back for the knob, except I was in his way, trying desperately not to fall on him. I fell, barely missing him. The cop, with his hands outstretched, took a quick glance at us and said, "Just stay right there, don't move."

The guys asked me after, why didn't you just run out, but I didn't know how to explain that I simply could not move. That I could feel every muscle, bone, and cell in me frozen in place. That my three-hundred-and-thirty-pound body was glued to the dirty vestibule floor, and never mind that Sr. Domingo was blocking the door.

The other cop, with the gun in his hand, seemed to suddenly realize there were other people there. He turned to us, gun pointing. I think I prayed at that moment. I'd seen guns, held a gun, and once playing around, shot a round, but I had never had a gun pointed directly at me. The barrel was the blackest black; it was a black hole pulling me in. I must have closed my eyes, for when I opened them, the light was bright, too bright, and the mailboxes looked like they were lopsided. I think I tried to get up and the cop with the surrender hands said, looking at me, "Don't move." I plopped back down. Sr. Domingo reached out a hand and put it on my chest. He tried to reassure me with his eyes, but he looked just as scared as I did. Marco was saying something, but I could barely make it out over the heartbeat in my ears. The gun-cop looked young like he was fresh out of high school. His face was red, and his dark hair was plastered to his forehead from sweat.

"What baby?" Gun-less cop said.

"The baby ... the baby is dead," said Marco. His voice cracked and sputtered. He was crying and screaming. I could see the gun shaking in his hand.

"It's her fault."

"What, who?"

It was then that I recognized the cop, Sgt. Ortiz. Everybody knew him, and he probably knew everyone in the neighborhood. The old ladies loved him. He seemed to know all their names. The little kids thought of him as some kind of superhero and some of the ladies, including my mother, were always a little extra friendly with him. He was tall, light brown, and kept a very sharp mustache. He knew me, the whole crew, and knew what we were up to; we prided ourselves on never getting caught. When Marco said the baby was born dead, Sgt. Ortiz was quiet for so long I'd thought that maybe I was dreaming all of it and everyone was frozen like a movie paused in mid-action. And then the white cop moved and I knew it was real. It was clear Sgt. Ortiz was thinking hard about what to say next. "Sometimes things like this happen."

And then everything both sped up and slowed down. Sgt. Ortiz was almost on Marco, his hand inches from the gun. I was holding my breath, waiting and hoping. So focused were we that no one noticed the elevator coming down from the fifth floor.

"I miss him."

Sgt. Ortiz nodded.

I don't know why the gun cop thought that was a good time to talk, to show off some level of expertise that no one needed or asked for.

"Yes, sometimes nature determines that a fetus is not viable."

Both Sgt. Ortiz and Marco looked at him. In my mind, I screamed, shut up! I could see the color rising on Marco's face. To be fair, Sgt. Ortiz and gun cop didn't know Marco could be sweet one second and put a knife to your throat the next because you laughed at him, defied him in some way, or simply said something he didn't like or agree with. They couldn't see that Marco's temper was at its tipping point. When Marco was already so hype and tight, you didn't ask questions, you didn't probe; you gave him all the room in the world. You stayed the hell away from him. We had a code when Marco was like that: 6911. If 6911 came on my beeper—the six was the M on the phone pad, followed by 911—it meant Marco had lost his shit and was looking to aim his anger at someone. But they didn't know that; they didn't know Marco as I did.

"Motherfucker," Marco started yelling. "Motherfucker," and he pointed the gun first to his temple and then toward the cop.

"Noooooo!" Sgt. Ortiz screamed. The elevator dinged as its door slid open, Marco's aunt, Doña Flores, came out as the gun cop shot once, then twice.

For a moment, I thought Sgt. Ortiz was reaching out to hug him, and it looked like Marco was extending his arms to receive him. Doña Flores and Sgt. Ortiz caught Marco as he fell to the ground. Doña Flores was screaming, crying, yelling, a sound so full of pain just the thought of it now still gives me chills.

Sgt. Ortiz kept saying, "Marco, Marco, Marco."

Doña Flores screamed, "Mi hijo, mi hijo, mi hijo," and I balled myself as tight as I could and cried. And then suddenly, there was a loud bang on the door, and a throng of cops rushed in. All I saw was an endless sea of blue legs and black shoes.

Gun cop stood by Sgt. Ortiz as he and Doña Flores held onto Marco. Sgt. Ortiz barked orders at the cops that rushed in. A few got on their radios; a couple of the others moved the gun cop back and gently took the gun from him. When they did that, he leaned against the wall and looked all of three years old, put in the corner for time out. They were talking to him, trying to get his attention, but all he could do was stare at Marco.

Marco's face was turned in my direction; his eyes blinked and seemed to swirl in their sockets until he found my face. He stared and stared at me. Doña Flores sat by him, her yellow skirt absorbing the blood coming out of Marco's chest and head. A female cop knelt down near her and spoke to her quietly, trying to convince her to get up. Doña Flores wasn't leaving her baby, she said. Doña Flores shooed away the female cop like a fly. Two other cops attempted to lift her up. They found her surprisingly strong for a small old lady; as they pulled her up, and she pulled away and sat back down. In the end, the EMT team just worked around her; when they put Marco on the gurney to wheel him out, she stood with her yellow skirt stained pink and red and followed them out.

I don't know how long I sat there; my arms wrapped around my knees. Marco's vacant eyes kept staring at me long after he was gone. Suddenly there was a bright light in my eyes, and I tried to move away. The EMT was saying something, but I couldn't hear him; my ears were ringing. I pushed his hand away and turned to see where Sr. Domingo was. He stood with the help of an officer, but he was shaking so hard they made him sit back down.

And then, all at once, I could hear everything—voices, sirens, yelling, and crying. The doors to the building were open, and I could hear the neighborhood, their voices combining and coming into the building, rushing in like a loud whisper. I looked back through the glass, and there was a swarm of people standing out there. They must have been watching through the glass. I saw my mother and Sr. Domingo's wife clinging to each other. At some point, some cops helped me up and walked me through the side door, which I was grateful for. I didn't want to face my mother or anybody else. As they walked me out, I saw Sgt. Ortiz grunting and pounding the wall, surrounded by three cops while gun cop stood still in his time out with an ashen face.

All of that happened in less than five minutes. It was the most unbelievable thing I had ever heard. Iggy told me that he and Chico wanted to get into the building, but by the time they got there, the cops were driving their cars onto the plaza. A few cops immediately jumped out of their cars. Iggy smiled and almost laughed as he told this to me. "The closest we could get," he continued, "was in front of the small shrine for the Virgen de Guadalupe."

Little Joey, not to be confused with Big Joey or Skinny Joey, who actually was tall and skinny, kept yelling out what was happening. And people on the terraces across the way had the best view. "We pushed our way through as best we could, but all we saw was the top of your head, and then we heard the shot and then the other one," Iggy continued. I had to put my hand up so he could shut up. Iggy continued to smile and walk in a circle, waiting, his black clothes always immaculate, and Chico, always quiet, kept his eyes on me while leaning against the building. He wore five gold chains on top of white t-shirts, and his jeans were creased so sharply they looked like they could cut you. They expected me to fill in the gaps, but I couldn't talk about it and just walked away. I don't think any of them knew how terrified I was or how sad and angry Marco was or how loud that bullet sounded and resounded in my head. None of them knew.

When I got home that night, my mom helped me out of my clothes. It was a funny sight: she, this tiny woman, helping her big fat son out of his clothes and into bed. Once in bed, she sat by me. I wasn't yet ready to face her, so I turned to face the wall. I heard the click of the lighter, the quick inhale, and the sweet smell of a freshly lit cigarette. She rubbed my back and said, "I was so scared. I heard those gunshots and almost fell to my knees. And didn't really know how I was going to live without you." Her voice was raw from crying.

The next morning, I walked into the kitchen where my mother sat smoking a cigarette and drinking her tea so dark, it looked like coffee. I sat across from her with downcast eyes.

"Pedro Daniel Alvaro me han dicho cosas de ti, and I'm having a hard time believing them." At the mention of my whole name, I quickly looked up at her and then down again. "Is it true what they say about you? At first, I said no, no, not my son. He wouldn't. Is it true?"

I nodded and slowly told my mother everything. Everything. I showed her my stash of cash. It wasn't a lot, less than a thousand dollars.

"Why?" Her voice had lost its rawness from the night before.

"I don't know."

"It wasn't for food? Because you never starved. So you didn't have the best sneakers or the nicest clothes, but you could have taken your ass to work."

I looked incredulously at her.

"Oh, you're too good to work? Is that what you're saying? I clearly failed you. Because I've done nothing but work hard, in jobs that I thought I was too good for, but I thought my son needs to eat, a home, so I'll take this job working ten hours a day in a factory, making clothes that I probably can't afford to wear, and yes, I'll work on the weekend, cleaning rich people's houses so that I can give my son the things he needs, if not everything he wants. And for what, la verguenza ..." She said all this quickly, then took a long drag of her Marlboro Light, closed her eyes, and exhaled. When she looked at me again, tears slid down her face. "Do you owe anyone money? Is this all your money?"

"This is all mine," I said, my hands shaking.

"Ven," she said as I followed her back into my room. "Besides this, what else do you have?" she said, holding the sneaker box with money.

I had three chains: one silver with a diamond-encrusted cross and two thick gold link ones. She looked at me, her face hard, and rolled her eyes. "Which one do you want to keep?" I pointed to the diamond one. She put the gold chains in the pocket of her house dress.

"What else do you have?"

I opened my closet and pointed to six shoeboxes; three had Timberlands, and the other three were Jordans. She looked at my jeans, some new ones with the price tags still on them; she checked the prices and raised her eyebrows.

"You will have to live with these clothes for a long time."

Before I could say anything, she left the room and quickly came back. She handed me the rent receipt. It was four hundred and forty dollars. "Give me half, right now." I opened the box in her arms and counted two hundred and twenty dollars.

"I expect you to give me half of the rent from now on. And if you continue selling drugs, I will throw you out and never look back." She grabbed my chin, pulled my face down, and made me look at her. "Do you understand?" I nodded.

She counted what was left in the box, gave me a hundred and fifty dollars, and said save it. "Tomorrow, you are going to offer Eva and her grandmother money to help with the funeral costs." My eyes widened. "After that, we're going to the supermarket, and you're going to buy this month's food. It's about time you learned the value of money."

And that was that. I could have sneaked around and set up with another crew, but I didn't. It's hard to see someone you know get shot and die. It was also hard to see your mother's love turn to distrust and disgust.

If I had been having second thoughts about getting my shit together, going to two funerals in one week was enough to make the choice clear-cut. I could get no closer to Marco's body than I could to his son's. The mere mention of Marco's name and I saw his vacant eyes as the blood pooled around him. Lorenzo came away from both funerals like a broken old man. We tried to hang out after that, but it was hard. I was working nights. Sr. Domingo pulled some strings and got me a job at his old factory. We didn't talk about Eva or Marco, although if Lorenzo had asked me what happened, I would have told him. He never did.

This morning, I want to see the old neighborhood. I walk around the boulevard, and although the store names have changed, everything is remarkably the same—there is still the discount houseware store, the discount children's clothing store, the discount sneaker-jean store, and the discount ladies stores. The diner, the old lady lingerie store, and KFC are all gone. The Korean grocers are still there, although their place seems smaller. I walk onto the old block via 163rd Street. I can't keep the smile off my face, despite how things ended; this is where I spent my youth.

I walk past the old parking lot that is now closed and past what we used to call the Mexican buildings. The majority of the families that lived in the small tenements were Mexican. I see that there is now an even larger mural of la Virgen de Guadalupe, and at her feet are half-burned candles and a mixture of real and plastic flowers. She's beautiful and regal and faces the plaza.

The orange brick on my old building is a little faded. I instinctively look up at the terraces, hoping to see familiar faces. Sr. Domingo and his wife left soon after the shooting. I wonder who lives there now, and just like back then, the terraces are filled with all kinds of stuff: plants, chairs, tables, decorations. They were and are extensions of people's living rooms. I can smell both pernil and habichuelas and want to laugh out loud. Man, I've missed this place.

I walk past the basketball courts that are now locked and the bodega that is owned by Arabs and go to the local bakery and get a coffee, a little dark with no sugar and a half-loaf of soft, hot, buttery bread. I sit on the cement benches in front of the basketball courts with a goofy grin. The first girl I ever kissed was Marisol, on the other side of the court. We were both a bit drunk and high, and I remember thinking as I kissed her that she tasted like bubble gum. As I was driving myself here, I wondered why I was coming back; what or who was I looking for? It would be great to see Lorenzo, just to see his pale face always hidden under a Yankees baseball cap. It would be nice to shoot the shit and catch up. I've missed him.

We lost touch so abruptly all those years ago. A week after Marco's funeral, Lorenzo told me that he and his aunt were moving to Parkchester. It wasn't that far, but back then, that was a whole lifetime away. It might be good to get away, I had said. Yeah, he responded, glancing over at

Eva's terrace, whose door was wide open. Just then Eva had stepped out, looked around, and threw a yellow plastic tub on the ground. We looked at each other and then back up at the terrace. We heard her scream, and then there she was again with something else in her hand. Whatever it was she threw this time cracked when it landed on the cement sidewalk. People on the street stopped and stared and folks came out on their terraces to see what was happening. Again, she screamed and came back out and threw something else. Each time she came back out, I thought for just a second that she was going to climb over the railing and throw herself off. She held whatever it was in her hand and flung it with such ferocity you could actually see the rail shake.

From behind me came Doña Elli, who had been visiting Doña Anita, known to us as the cake lady. She dashed across the plaza into Eva's building. Eva came out one more time. She watched a bunch of diapers as they floated to the ground. Lorenzo also headed toward the building; he looked back at me. I couldn't decipher the look on his face. Did he need courage, or did he want me to go? I couldn't give him either. He turned away and ran toward the building, following Doña Elli. I waited and watched. Eva had stopped screaming, and I saw Lorenzo close the terrace door.

The baby clothes, toys, bottles, diapers, and small yellow plastic tub were scattered across the plaza like large pieces of confetti, brightly colored and sparkly. No one touched any of it. Drunk Esperanza walked a mumble-less wide arch around them. Finally, Doña Anita came out and picked up the tiny baby clothes one by one, shook the dirt off, and placed it gently in the yellow tub. When she dusted off each item, you could see that some were blue for boys and others pink and frilly for girls. The broken bottles and toys she put in the trash bin by the basketball courts, and then she headed upstairs toward Eva.

That was the last time I saw Lorenzo. My mother told me the next morning that Eva had gone to the hospital. I beeped Lorenzo, but he never called or beeped me back.

I finish my coffee and look at a mural on the bodega wall of a young man's face, surrounded by clouds. The year of his birth, 1998, and the year of his death, 2015, below his name, Jorge Garcia Jr. Either the anniversary of his birth or death had just occurred, for there was one tall white glass-encased candle still lit. I didn't know him, but I could have, and I probably knew and was a version of him—a young man confusing bravery with recklessness.

It's early on a Saturday morning, and the only folks out are either rushing off to work or the old folks are headed to the supermarket or the bank to avoid long lines. I ask myself again, why am I here? Marco is dead. Lorenzo has long been gone, and I never did find out what happened to Eva. I want to know that they are okay; I also want to let them know that I am okay too. I'm about to start my own family and wanted to share the news with them. I've been married for a year, and my wife, Christina, and I are expecting our first baby. I've thought about how old Eva and Marco's son would be by now, fifteen, sixteen maybe? What if he had lived? Where would Marco be? Where would Lorenzo be? I know for sure that this life that I have now would not be possible if that baby had lived. It's a terrible discovery to make.

I walk to my old building's entrance. The bottom half of the window and door are dark brown plastic but used to be all glass. I think about being in the vestibule with Sr. Domingo and those two cops and how the echo of those two shots has never stopped reverberating in my life. Maybe whatever it is I'm looking for can't really be found. I'm looking for some way to resolve the past and tuck it away.

"Pedro," I hear a voice call out.

I turn to see Doña Anita, tall and pretty as ever. Her white hair is cropped short and looks beautiful against her black skin. She's hugging me before I can even say her name.

"Look at you," she says. "Look at you!" She steps back while still holding my hand and smiles. "You look good." I smile right back and throw my arm around her shoulders. Seeing her suddenly makes the whole trip worthwhile. She takes me upstairs to her apartment. It still smells like sugar and cinnamon. It reminds me of coming after school and buying thick pieces of cake from her. She makes me sit in the living room while she fusses in the kitchen.

"I saw your mother a few years ago on the bus. She told me you were doing well. That you had finished school and you are an engineer." Her smile is big, and she looks at me through the kitchen cut-away and then goes back to what she was doing.

"Yes," I say shyly.

"She is so proud of you. Is she okay?"

"Yeah, she's good; she's about to retire soon." Saying that makes me wonder how old Doña Anita is. She must be in her eighties.

"You're lucky," she says. "I think this was your favorite, the yellow cake with chocolate frosting."

I smile. It was.

She puts a piece of cake on a small paper plate and gives me a plastic fork. She leaves and comes back holding a coffee cup with a faded flower design on it filled with black coffee. "Do you need sugar?"

"No," I say. I'm not sure I could eat the cake, but you never turn down food; that much is still true. I taste the cake; it is moist, and the chocolate frosting is tooth-achingly sweet. "It's just like I remember." In between bites, I ask her about Sr. Domingo and Doña Elli.

"Ah, Domingo, he died two summers ago. Cancer." She's silent for a long time before continuing. "Elli is fine, old like me, with old folks' worries and pains."

"I always thought he was such a nice man."

"He was. There was plenty to love and plenty not to." She half-smiles when she says that and looks out toward the terrace door. "I made a cake for the girls, their granddaughters, my god babies. I'm going to see them later today. Elli will be so happy I saw you. We talk about you often."

I am surprised to hear that.

"We think about all the young people we've seen grow up and move out," she says as though answering my unasked question. "This will make her day."

"Do you know anything about Eva or Lorenzo?" I ask, hoping.

She pats my hand. Hers are amazingly soft. Then she picks up my empty cup to take back to the kitchen. As she stands, she mentions, "I don't know anything about Lorenzo. When they moved, it was the last I saw him." She puckers her lips after she speaks. "Eva is fine." Her voice is low. "She lives, oh, where does she live? I think I have her address; let me see if I can find it for you." She puts the cup back down and heads toward the back.

Before I can say anything else, she is off in her bedroom, looking for the address. I am glad to hear about Eva and disappointed that there is no news about Lorenzo. She comes back with a folded envelope. "Eva sends me and Elli Christmas cards every year." She hands it to me and keeps talking. "She's good. She has a two-year-old daughter who's very adorable. I had a picture of her, but I don't know where I put it. Anyway, she's fine." Her voice loses its cheeriness. "After...you know, after, it took her some time to recover. Ellie and I would go visit her, help Celeste take care of her. Very slowly, she got better. You see her now and you think, what a lovely young woman. Do you remember Francisco?" she asks me before taking my plate into the kitchen.

"Francisco?"

"Yes, the skinny boy. You used to hang out with him. You and Lorenzo, he wore black all the time."

"Iggy," I say, smiling.

"Iggy? Qué es Iggy?"

I laugh. That's what we used to call him, I tell her. She shakes her head in disbelief. "He lives on the other side of Simpson, near Casita Maria. He's still skinny and still wears black. He does some kind of mechanical work in the old factory where Domingo worked. I think after Marco was killed, Domingo tried to get all you boys a job." She crosses herself at the mention of Marco.

"Sr. Domingo got me a job."

She nods, remembering.

"Do you know which building? Iggy...Francisco lives in?"

"Ay no, no, but I see him a lot. I can give him your number."

She rips the flap off the folded envelope and says, "Write it down here." She gets up slowly and goes back into the kitchen for a pen.

I come down an hour later after promising to return with Christina. I take one look around, step down into the plaza, and feel more at peace. I've felt guilty about moving on. I want to know that Lorenzo has survived not just this place, but also the baby and Marco's death. Maybe I'll never know about Lorenzo, but the news about Eva being happy and a mother brings me tremendous relief.

I stopped wondering what I could have done. It's not like I had any power. The fight between Marco and Lorenzo was an old one. I didn't understand the push and pull, love and hate, and rivalry that exists between siblings.

Standing in the plaza, imagining my eighteen-year-old self trying to do something selfless and meaningful, was at odds with who I was back then. The smell of pernil is thick in the air. Little kids are out riding their bikes, enjoying the last of the fall weather. Salsa music wafts from one of the terraces, and there is a steady stream of customers coming and going from the bodega. A few guys have gathered by the memorial mural. I watch and recognize what they are doing, setting up for the day.

I'm glad it's not me.

I'm glad I got out.

ACKNOWLEDGMENTS

This book could not have happened without the support, encouragement, and love of family and friends.

First and foremost, I would like to thank Naomi Rosenblatt of Heliotrope Books, whose friendship and encouragment have been a sweet delight. None of this could have happened without your simple question: "Are you ready?"

When I think of family, I think of my tías, tíos, and cousins all gathered in my grandmother's tiny living room with our plates overflowing with food on Noche Buena, laughing, talking way too loud over the music, and eating. I miss you, Abuela, and I hope I've made you proud. Thank you, Pa, for your unconditional love. I wish we'd had more time to dance together. Thank you, Tía Carmen for giving me my first journal and encouraging me to write. To my second mother and secret keeper, Tía Inesita, thank you, for always being there. To my cousin Julio Cesar your hugs remind me of what love is. To my little big brother Lou, thank you for being my biggest cheerleader. To know my mother, Mireya, is to know how much she loves her family. Your love is a force. Gwenie Gwen, my mother-in-law, thanks for loving me and sharing endless cups of coffee. To my nieces Kymira and Jazmyne, thank you for bringing me joy and happiness (and anxiety). I'm blessed to have you all as my bedrock.

My friends remind me to fly, be free, and take up all the space, and for that, I'm so profoundly grateful. To my Jedi Coven — Lisa Fireman Dorhout and Janine Alpizar Salvador, there are no words to describe the depth and breadth of my love for you. To my wolf pack — Lana Garland, the big sister I always hoped for, dispensing wisdom, listening to my fears, thank you for always nudging me forward, and Thembisa Mshaka for being pure inspiration. You have taught me more about resilience than anyone should. To Anika Burt, my gemela, who has held the dream of this book with me for more than fifteen years, who has read every version of every story and always said, "I can't wait to read more." I'm so lucky to know, love and call you family.

When I think I've reached the pinnacle of friendships the universe said, but wait there is more! Thank you, Barbara Turk. No family decision is made without your wise counsel and love. From the moment I met you, Llanor Alleyne, I knew you were a friend. This book is a reflection of your belief in me, your keen editing, and your never-ending prodding and pushing for me to write and do better. I'm forever indebted to you. Phil Phillips your smile is all I ever need to feel better about myself and the world. Ogonnaya Newman Dotson thank you for the joy and laughter you bring to my life. Your friendship is a treasure.

Darcy Richie and Margarita Villa you make my life full. Lorena Estrella, Sherridon Poyer, my Landmark friends, Well-Read, Badly Behaved book club, my Sadie Nash crew, my Alix cousins, my younger siblings, Alex and Luis, and Dad, thank you all for your cheers and love. I am humbled by it.

To my love, Kimberly M. Sanders, your steadfast love is my north star. Thank you for listening to all my (sometimes wacky) ideas, for being my first reader, and most importantly for making sure I hold on to my dreams. You are home.

AUTHOR

Esther Alix is a Black Latina, the eldest child of Dominican immigrants. She is a native New Yorker who grew up in the South Bronx. She lives with her partner and dog in Brooklyn. *Stories of Gabriel* is her debut short story collection.